Jackie wrapped her legs around one of Leah's, bringing herself urgently against Leah's hips. Her own passion was frightening. She couldn't stop herself to wonder if Leah felt the same desperate need. She worried that her desire would repulse Leah, but she couldn't slow down. Her mind told her that she didn't know what to do, but her body knew. Her hands went to Leah's shirt again and when the buttons wouldn't give way she tore them.

About the Author

Karin Kallmaker was born in 1960 and raised by her loving, middle-class parents in California's Central Valley. The physician's Statement of Live Birth plainly declares, "Sex: Female" and "Cry: Lusty." Both are still true. Her genealogically minded father recently informed her that she is descended from Lady Godiva.

From a normal childhood and equally unremarkable public-school adolescence, she went on to obtain an ordinary Bachelor's degree from the California State University at Sacramento. At the age of 16, eyes wide open, she fell into the arms of her first and only sweetheart. Ten years later, after seeing the film *Desert Hearts*, her sweetheart descended on the Berkeley Public Library determined to find some of "those" books. "Rule, Jane" led to "Lesbianism—Fiction" and then on to book after self-affirming book by and about lesbians. These books were the encouragement Karin needed to forget the so-called "mainstream" and spin her first romance for lesbians. That manuscript became her first Naiad Press novel, *In Every Port*.

Karin now lives in the San Francisco Bay Area with that very same sweetheart; she is a one-woman woman. The happily-ever-after couple became Mom and Moogie to Kelson James in 1995 and Eleanor Delenn in 1997. They celebrate their twenty-third anniversary in 2000.

Fans of romantic supernatural and science fiction should investigate Karin's alter-ego, Laura Adams.

PAINTED MOON

BY KARIN KALLMAKER

THE NAIAD PRESS, INC.
2000

Printed in the United States of America on acid-free paper
First Edition
Second Printing June 1995
Third Printing January 1997
Fourth Printing April 1998
Fifth Printing April 2000

Edited by Christine Cassidy
Cover design by Bonnie Liss (Phoenix Graphics)
Typeset by Sandi Stancil

Library of Congress Cataloging-in-Publication Data

Kallmaker, Karin, 1960–
    Painted moon / Karin Kallmaker.
        p.   cm.
    ISBN 1-56280-075-2
    1. Lesbians—Fiction.   I. Title.
PS3561.A41665P34   1994
813'.54—dc20
                                            94-16242
                                                CIP

For Maria, Mother Moon
and
James A. Sherman, vaguely normal,
gone too soon

The Fifth is for Vision

1

A winter storm warning meant snow for Thanksgiving.

Leah found the idea of giving thanks ironic. She had little to be thankful for. Another gust of wind shook the windowpanes in the A-frame of the loft above them and Butch leaned her whole weight across the back of Leah's legs with a whimper.

"I know, girl," she said absently. She thumped Butch's side through the thick white fur. Somehow Butch always knew when provisions were running low. If she didn't get into town and back before the storm, they'd be eating canned baked beans for Thanksgiving and several days after that.

Leah looked forward to being snowed in. If Mother Nature kept her from the outside world for a few days, then for those days the isolation wasn't by her choice.

This was her second Thanksgiving without Sharla. She wondered when she'd stop counting. "C'mon, girl," she said. She pulled on her plaid parka and snow boots. The earlier she started out the more likely she wouldn't need chains to get back.

Butch didn't need any encouragement. She scrambled out the door ahead of Leah and when the truck door was open, she hauled all ninety-five pounds of her Alaskan Husky body into the passenger seat. When Leah slammed the door after her, Butch barked once.

"Okay, okay, I'm hurrying."

The drive into Bishop wasn't bad — the truck was more than heavy enough to stand a little wind. But when she came out of the market, the snow was coming down in small flurries. She quickly stashed the paper sacks onto the floorboard below Butch. Butch panted and licked her lips.

"If you so much as nibble at that turkey, you won't see a single drumstick." Leah didn't know why she'd gotten a turkey except that they were really cheap — the penny-wise aspect of her Brethren up-bringing stayed with her no matter what her current bank balance was. In the back of her mind she thought perhaps she'd set the table with an empty chair for Sharla. Maybe Sharla's spirit would visit. Maybe it would leave her feeling whole instead of

2

walking around like a ghost. As though she'd been the one who had drowned.

She made a quick stop at the post office. There were two letters and a parcel she had to collect at the window. One letter was from her mother. Leah wasn't sure she should read it. The other was from Maureen and Valentina, persistent friends who continued to write even when Leah didn't answer.

The return address on the parcel made Leah catch her breath. She scrubbed her parka sleeve over her eyes. Why hadn't she cancelled her standing instructions with the art supply house? Every time one of these boxes arrived, it was like a knife in the chest.

The flurries had thickened. She had to bend into the wind to keep the snow out of her face as she went back to the truck. Why was everything so hard? Leah slammed both fists on the steering wheel. The spark of fury dwindled as fast as it had flamed and she closed her eyes against unaccountable weariness.

Butch whined and gnawed on the sleeve of her parka. Leah shook her loose and tried to calm herself. The snow was coming down in a no-nonsense steady flow . . . she didn't have time for the luxury of grief.

2

Jackie leaned forward and peered anxiously through the windshield. She flipped the beams to high, but the wall of rain and sleet reflected the extra light into her already straining eyes. She still could see nothing farther ahead than another car length — maybe two. Wincing, she switched back to low beams and prayed the lines on the road would remain visible as rain continued to wash over the pavement. The turnoff for Bishop loomed out of the dark and she slowly bore to the right. She clutched the MG down into low gear as the road curved and then headed what felt like straight up where the rain would be snow. Next stop, six thousand feet.

There was nothing else to do but inch ahead and curse everyone responsible for her predicament. This surely couldn't be *her* fault, she thought. Oh no, you're not the one driving an old sports car in this weather. No, it was her mother's fault for guilt-tripping her into spending Thanksgiving with her nearest living relative — an aunt Jackie hadn't seen since she was a toddler. It was also Parker's fault for advising her to buy the used but sporty MG when she had really wanted something with 4-wheel drive. It was her boss's fault for keeping her an extra three hours beyond when she had wanted to leave work. It never failed — whenever she told him she needed to leave by a specific time, a deadline always came along and she felt guilty, harried and ill-used by the time she left. Mannings would refer to her untimely departure for weeks. *If you'd stayed another hour, you would know why the project changed . . .*

He would have kept her there until midnight if she hadn't given him The Look. The Look told Mannings she'd had enough of changing CAD specifications one at a time and, no, she would not do a new set of twelve color proofs for client X before she left. The Look said she was sick of ticky-tacky box condominium design, Mannings, and the last-minute rush jobs that were keeping her later and later in increasingly foul weather.

All she had said was that she would do it on Monday. He became all consideration suddenly, expressing concern about the long drive ahead of her and the weather. It would take a lot out of a gal, he had said, to undertake a six-hour drive up into some

5

pretty big mountains. Jackie gritted her teeth. He always paused before saying *gal* — she knew he still wanted to say *girl,* even if it was the nineties. She gave him The Look again and told him no, she did not think starting out tomorrow morning was better.

She clenched the wheel and cursed herself for being too much of a coward to tell him that if she'd had the early start she'd intended there wouldn't be a problem. She passed an elevation sign: 5,000 feet. And she was still heading up. She was certain she was lost. She reached to turn the heater up again but checked herself. It was up as far up as it would go. Half-frozen rain clung to her wipers. Another blast of freezing air worked its way around the ragtop and Jackie groped in her glove compartment for the thin driving gloves Parker had given her. They weren't lined, but they were better than nothing.

She braked at the top of the grade and was relieved to see lights of civilization through the smearing slush on her windshield. She increased speed and saw a sign that said she'd found Bishop. It was a small place and she was through it in a few minutes. There were no other people in sight and all the houses she passed looked hunkered down for the storm. She drove carefully along the highway and fought back a tremor of fear. The left-turn pocket her aunt had told her to take popped out of the glare after only a few minutes of tense driving and Jackie heaved a sigh of relief. It was only another ten minutes, her aunt had said. She decided that she could make it to her aunt's house.

Of course, her aunt hadn't known it would be snowing. There were no street lights. City girl, she chided herself, you've gotten soft. Her MG wasn't made for this weather, she knew, but she had no choice except to press ahead. The snow thinned as she slowly ground her way up another grade. As the odometer clicked forward each tenth of a mile, she guessed that her aunt's ten-minute estimate might be a half-hour at this pace.

Her fear and doubts returned in full force when she crested the first grade. She hadn't realized it had been sheltering her from the wind and the worst of the snow. The MG shuddered when the initial blast of Arctic air hit it and snow immediately glazed her windshield. She sacrificed the warmth of her feet and turned all the heat onto the windshield. It helped, a little. She slowed to a crawl and guided the car from mileage marker to marker, grateful she could tell where the side of the road was.

The landscape appeared to stand still while the minutes clicked by. Jackie was beginning to feel as though she would end up in Brigadoon. The snow had already masked any landmark she might have recognized. She had left Bishop behind almost a half-hour ago. It had been almost eight hours since she had left San Francisco. She was cramped from concentrating and shivering. Her need for a bathroom was becoming acute, which wasn't helping her composure any. At times like this she envied Parker that handy little gadget he had.

Aunt Eliza would be frantic. They'd spoken briefly this morning and her aunt had told her to expect "a little rain." She hadn't known Jackie was driving a sports car into an Arctic storm.

The windshield wipers slapped ineffectually across the windshield — go back, go back, they seemed to say. Why hadn't they said that an hour ago? She wasn't sure she could turn around and not end up off the road. And where would she go back to? The only light was her headlights. The snowflakes were like Boston's in February — the type that slip inside your boots, no matter how tightly they're laced, and then melt instantly. The type of snow that tires slip on.

As if on cue, the MG slid sideways a few feet as Jackie slowly maneuvered it around a curve. Oh terrific, she thought as she brought the car out of the skid. *I wanted to buy something sensible, something I could take on a construction site if I had to, but no. Parker said the MG will be cute. Fun for us to take to the beach.* He had always wanted a convertible. They'd been to the beach exactly once in the last nine months.

Aunt Eliza had said that if she stayed on this road she'd come to a right turn. Then she was to drive without turn-offs to the second gate, and then she'd be on a gravel and dirt road. Gravel and dirt meant mud. The MG wasn't up to mud. It wasn't up to the asphalt and snow either. Every few feet the tires slid in the slush and then the car jolted as it plowed into packed snow. The unpredictable slide-thunk rhythm put her stomach in knots. She should just go back to Bishop and see if there was a motel with a vacancy. Or drive on a few hours north to Lake Tahoe. *Oh, right, Jackie. Like you could get to Tahoe in this weather.*

I am a fool, she cursed herself. She slowed the car and listened to the disarmingly quiet *plop-plop* of snow on the ragtop. There was nothing for it. It was a long climb up the hill she'd just come down, and probably another forty minutes to get back to Bishop, but she didn't think she would see a gate or a road in this weather, and she would freeze to death in the MG if the engine died. She had to turn back.

She began the treacherous Y-turn. If there was any traffic, they'd run right into her. She also couldn't see clearly enough to tell if she'd turned the full 180 degrees. *Where is the marker I just passed?* The sleet made it nearly invisible . . . there.

She let out the clutch and the MG shuddered its way back up the hill. At the crest, Jackie steered slowly to the left. It took her a few seconds to realize that the MG was heading to the right. She wrenched the wheel harder with no effect, then pumped the brakes lightly, then more frantically as the car continued to slowly slip sideways on the slope of the road. The right wheels dropped onto the shoulder and the car picked up speed as it slid completely off the pavement and tipped down the slope.

Jackie had a split-second to decide if she should unbuckle her seat belt and try to jump out of the car or if she should stay with the car and hope the seat belt would somehow save her from injury. But then the car slowed, and with a mild jolt, it stopped.

Jackie opened her eyes. They were lodged against a row of sturdy pine trees only about four feet below the road. It could have been much, much worse.

The snow was light under the trees but even as Jackie decided to stay where she was the MG's engine gave a wheezy splutter and died. She gingerly tried to coax it back to life. She tried swearing. Neither approach worked. It was probably the angle . . . gas couldn't reach the engine. She thought bitterly of the used Trooper she had wanted to buy and the Trooper's fuel injection system, heater, anti-lock brakes and on-demand 4-wheel drive.

The temperature in the car fell rapidly. Jackie blew on her fingers and decided she'd have to get out and walk. Walking would keep her warm, which was vital, and she knew her aunt's house lay ahead. She didn't know how far, but she would get there.

The next most important thing was to keep her feet dry. She had on her thickest leather boots . . . not hiking boots by any stretch of the imagination, but they were warm and waterproof. They'd survived a Boston winter. With some scrambling she managed to fish her suitcase out from behind the seat. She added a second pair of jeans over the ones she wore — the big jeans she'd brought for after the Thanksgiving meal — then pulled two oversized sweaters over the pullover she was already wearing. She struggled back into her jacket, another Boston survivor.

She stuffed extra underpants and socks into her jacket pockets, thinking she would wrap them around her hands if she had to, and she cursed herself for not throwing in a wool scarf or a pair of real gloves. Her jacket didn't have a hood and she needed to preserve what she could of her body heat. Her braid would help, but she didn't have bobby pins. She piled her braid around the top of her head and wrapped a sweater vest around it like a ski mask. A silk scarf secured it in place, sort of. Her thickest socks became mittens over the driving gloves. She was never more grateful that she used a fanny pack instead of a purse. She strapped it around her and had the morbid thought that if she froze to death her driver's license would identify her body. As the emergency card in her wallet said, the nearest Canadian embassy could find her father almost immediately.

Her movements were stiff through all the layers, but the cold didn't immediately hit her when she got out of the car. That was a good sign, she thought. She peered through one armhole of the vest and scrambled as best she could up the sodden, slippery hillside. Wetness had penetrated to her hands and knees by the time she reached the road.

On foot she had a decent chance of seeing a gate, so she headed down the grade in the direction she thought her aunt's house lay. Surely they would be looking for her ... or maybe they thought she'd had the sense to stop when it got bad. Don't panic, she told herself. *This isn't any worse than when you and Mom got trapped at the top of the ski run at Banff. It's no worse than any survival-training vacation Dad dragged us on.* She would write him the moment she got home and thank him for insisting she learn some basics.

By the time she reached the top of the next grade, her nose and ears were numb and she was sweating profusely under the sweaters. Her lungs ached from the cold and lack of oxygen. At the bottom of the hill, surely there would be houses. There had to be. The idea of climbing another hill ... her heart sank. She paused for a moment and heard a faint whine behind her.

In a panic of hope, she moved to the side of the road, though she could tell that the vehicle was moving slowly. Headlights finally appeared and she stepped into the pools of light, waving frantically.

It was a pick-up, a big one. The kind that rednecks drove on television. It probably had gun racks. As the truck stopped, a huge white dog lunged at the passenger-side window, baring its teeth. Jackie jumped back.

The passenger door flew open. A hoarse voice ordered the dog to stay, then rasped at her, "Are you trying to get yourself killed?"

Jackie didn't know what to say. Killed how? Freezing? Rabies? Getting run over by a surly hick? Everything she'd ever been taught about the consequences of accepting rides from strangers surged inside her. City survival tactics applied now, she told herself, then realized she was near hysterics. "My car went off the road. If you could call my —"

"Will you get in before we both freeze?"

"I don't need a lift — "

"Suit yourself." The door started to close.

"No, wait!" Jackie grabbed the door and heedless of the dog, stepped up onto the running board. She dragged the sweater vest off her head and tossed her braid back, peering anxiously at the driver. She could make out nothing more than a thick flannel jacket — the kind that hunters wore. But no sign of a gun rack. "If you could call my aunt —"

"I don't have a cellular phone," the driver said sarcastically, leaning toward Jackie. As the overhead light illuminated short, dark hair and thin, ascetic features, Jackie realized the driver was a woman. She nearly fainted with relief.

The woman said, "Just get in, will you? Butch doesn't bite and neither do I."

3

What had she done to deserve this? Leah gunned the engine and wasn't surprised when Butch sidled up against her. Idiot woman was drizzling water all over the inside of the truck. The paper bags were going to get wet and they'd be chasing canned peas down the driveway.

God spare her from people who thought the weather could be reasoned with. Nothing made Mother Nature more vicious than when her power was taken for granted. Going back to town was unthinkable. She'd slid twice on the last grade, and her own gate was just a half a mile ahead. She'd be damned if she'd put on chains when she was so close to home. She was going to have the last thing she wanted for Thanksgiving — a visitor.

She pulled up in front of the gate and started to open her door, but the woman said, "I'll get it," and slipped out. Well, maybe she had some sense after all even if she did look seventeen with that braid. Leah watched her stumble through the snow ... *oh hell, look at those boots.* Where did this fool think she'd been headed? Club Med?

The woman managed the gate catch and held it open as Leah drove through. In the rear view mirror Leah saw the woman latch it again properly and then disappear as she stumbled. When she opened the door she was covered with slushy snow. Butch moved halfway onto Leah's lap.

The woman didn't say anything, though. Leah muttered, "Hang on," and started her descent down the steepest driveway in the whole Mammoth Lakes area. It put off casual callers, something that suited Leah just fine. Snow was already piling up against the garage door, so putting the truck in there was out of the question. She pulled onto the intermediate plateau above the house and said, "We'll have to walk down. Carry as much as you can. Maybe we won't have to make another trip."

As Leah had expected, the paper bags tore when they picked them up. The woman shrugged out of her jacket and piled groceries into it without comment, then staggered down the hill fully loaded. She lost her footing near the bottom and slid the last few feet on her butt, landing against the drift accumulating against the garage. Her expression was such a funny mix of chagrin and annoyance that Leah felt like laughing — something she hadn't done for quite some time. But she had to admire her pluck; she picked herself out of the snow without exclamation or assistance and trudged up the steps.

"Now look, I'm trusting you with this," Leah said to Butch. "You have to behave. We have company." She extended the plastic handle of the turkey's mesh bag toward Butch. Butch solemnly clenched the handle between her front teeth and obediently dragged the plastic-wrapped turkey down the snow-covered slope to the house.

Using her jacket the same way the woman had, Leah was able to haul in the last of the groceries. She had misplaced the art supply box somewhere along the way, but that didn't bother her one bit, she thought as she dumped the bundle unceremoniously on the kitchen floor. She realized that Butch was now eyeing the turkey lustfully, so she removed it to a safer place in the back porch sink. "Turn up the fire," she said over her shoulder.

When she came back into the kitchen, the woman was huddled near the stove. A pile of sodden clothing on the floor was growing as the woman yanked first one sweater, then another over her head and let it fall. "I n-need something to wear," she said. "I'm w-wet all the way through."

Leah went into the spare room. Underneath all the layers of clothing had been a small-boned but well-filled-out woman. Sharla's clothes would be a better fit, she decided. Her own sweaters were too narrow in the shoulders and hips. She held a thick New Zealand wool sweater against her face for a moment, remembering the feel of it with Sharla's soft, exquisite body underneath. She shuddered violently, her longing for Sharla flaring up through her spine. She knew she had to stop feeling like this.

She gave herself a moment to regain her composure, then went back to the kitchen.

The woman accepted the sweater, underthings and corduroy pants without comment, then asked where the bathroom was. Leah pointed it out and the woman hurried away.

♥ ♥ ♥ ♥ ♥

Well, this was the most awkward situation she'd ever been in, Jackie thought. Trapped in a winter cabin with a dour mountain woman about as sociable as her dog. "Turn the fire up." As if Jackie would play with a wood burning stove without instructions.

Be nice, she told herself. This woman has saved you from freezing to death. She shuddered into the clothes and patted her hair, wondering if she should undo the braid so it could dry. No, it looked halfway decent as it was. She went back to the kitchen, thinking of the heat coming from the kitchen stove.

"I feel almost human. Thank you," she said as she entered. Her rescuer looked up from poking inside the stove and immediately looked away. Jackie stealthily checked her fly . . . it was buttoned. It was as though Mountain Woman couldn't stand the sight of her. "I'm really sorry to be imposing on you like this. Do you know how far it is to the Carson place?"

"About a mile and a half."

"Oh. I thought maybe I could walk it." She kept

me from freezing, Jackie reminded herself. *I might not have made it.*

"Don't be stupid."

Pleased to meet you, too, Jackie thought. *The least she could do is look at me.* "I know that's out of the question now. I got a late start. I should have been there hours ago. My boss kept me late. In San Francisco." She realized she was babbling. A near-death experience wasn't exactly calming.

"Phone's on the wall. It might still work."

"Oh. Thanks." *Okay, we'll keep it to short sentences.* Her relatives could come get her in the morning. She dug her fanny pack out from under her wet clothes and fished out her aunt's phone number. The connection crackled, then the call went through.

Her aunt, no doubt expecting the phone service to stop at any moment, launched into speech as soon as she heard Jackie's voice. "I've been worried sick. The weather service just didn't do justice ta this storm. It's a doozy. Your mother'd have my hide if something happened ta you. Where are you?"

"I'm at one of your neighbors. My car slipped off the road." Her aunt gasped in alarm. "No, I'm okay. Nothing even bruised." Except her rear end, but that had happened when she'd fallen down with the groceries. She turned to her rescuer who was dropping kindling and small logs into the stove. "Where am I?"

"At the old McCormick place."

She repeated the information to her aunt who gave a small gasp. "Oh, Jackie, maybe Hank can come ta get you . . . no, he's shaking his head. But I hate ta think of you there."

Jackie heard the emphasis on the last word. Had she fallen in with the local bootleg gin manufacturer? Or a modern day Lizzie Borden? Her aunt most definitely disapproved. "I'm fine, really. My hostess has been very considerate."

"I'll bet," her aunt said. "You just watch out for yourself. Hank'll be there soon as the weather breaks. Should be tamorra morning some —"

The line went dead.

Jackie tried calling back but there was no dial tone, so she gave up. "My uncle will pick me up when the weather breaks, Ms. McCormick."

The woman actually smiled ... slightly. "I'm Leah Beck. I own it now, but this cabin will always be the McCormick place."

"Sorry. Well, I can't tell you how glad I am you came along. I had no intention of being out in this kind of weather in a sports car." Leah rolled her eyes and Jackie felt stupid, so she defended herself. "It was my boyfriend's idea. I wanted to buy something a little more utilitarian than an MG."

"Who are you?" Leah put the cover back over the fire and turned to face her as though braving herself to do it. Jackie wondered if she frightened Leah.

"Oh, sorry. Jackie Frakes."

"Any relation?"

Jackie blinked. Not very many people associated her name with her mother's. "To whom?"

"The sculptor."

Jackie blinked. This antisocial, eccentric woman knew her mother's work? "Yes, she's my mother."

Leah winced, then began picking up the groceries. Jackie bent to help her. "That's okay," Leah said. "I can do it."

"I'm sure you can, but I need to do something to earn my keep."

"Do something about your clothes. There's clothespins in the drawer closest to the stove. They'll all be dry in no time."

Jackie gathered she was to hang them on the thin wire behind the stove. She examined it, discovered it had a clever pulley system, and hung everything up, including the sodden panties from her jeans' pockets. The heat coming off the stove was fierce and oh, so comforting. Jackie finally felt some sensation in her earlobes.

"Have you had any dinner?"

"Just a Big Mac about five hours ago," Jackie said. "I grabbed one as I went through Vacaville."

"I was planning to heat up some leftover stew."

"Sounds great." As if on cue, her stomach growled. Butch's head jerked toward her. "Nice doggy," she said. She'd never been great with animals; her father's work had kept them moving around too much to have pets.

"If you call her a doggy she'll bite you," Leah said. She turned away, but Jackie still saw a trace of a smile.

"Why Butch for a girl?"

Leah kept her back turned. "Because she acts really tough, but when you get her on her back, she's a pussycat." There was something between laughter and pain in her voice.

Strange name, Jackie thought as she held out her fingers. After a moment, Butch deigned to sniff them. Then she nudged them with her nose. Jackie scratched slightly and was rewarded by Butch sinking lower and lower until she was on the floor. She stroked Butch's side and Butch rolled over with a sigh. She closed her eyes when Jackie scratched her stomach.

"I see what you mean."

Leah set a saucepan on the stove and went back to putting the groceries away as if Jackie didn't exist. Within a few minutes Jackie could hear the stew bubbling, so she got up to stir it. Leah noticed her existence enough to tell her where bowls and spoons were and then passed her a loaf of bread and a long-handled fork. Hah, thought Jackie. *I'll bet she thinks I don't know what a toasting fork is. She doesn't know Daddy and his fondness for wilderness holidays.*

Leah didn't remark on the nicely browned toast Jackie produced from over the stove. She had been tempted to butter it while on the fork and then let it sizzle for just a few moments on the hot stove top, but that would be showing off. The stew was surprisingly good and it chased the last of her snow experience away. She wondered what on earth she and Leah would talk about. It was hard to have a conversation with someone who was as moody as hell. Butch was starting to look like the better conversationalist of the two.

Leah pulled on her parka and boots and left Jackie to the dirty dishes she insisted on doing. Suddenly, all the lights flickered. Jackie told Leah when she came back in the house.

"They do that when you turn the generator on. We're going to lose the electric before the night's out. The propane tank is full — we could last a couple of weeks." She stomped her feet on the floor, scattering ice and snow, then kicked her boots off. "Do you like classical music?"

"Baroque, rococo or romance?"

"All of the above." Leah actually did smile. Jackie was surprised and pleased. Leah seemed to warm up with time.

Jackie made short work of the dishes, but there had only been a few. She trailed after Leah, who was programming a couple of CDs into the player. A lovely Bach suite swirled out of the speakers. "Very civilized," Jackie said.

"Isn't it." Leah bent to stoke up the Franklin stove. "It'll warm up pretty quickly."

Jackie rubbed her arms. "It's amazing that it's so cold in here when the kitchen is so warm." The high ceiling was a classic A-frame with sky lights on either side. A loft took up the rear portion of the ceiling area. In the winter, Jackie was willing to bet it was toasty. In the summer the open skylights would bring a breeze across it.

Leah cleared her throat. "Look, um, there's only one bed and that's in the loft. It gets heat from the kitchen flue. I wouldn't mind if we shared...it's king-sized."

Jackie could tell that the idea bothered Leah a lot. "I can bunk down here on the couch. It's warming up already."

"By three a.m. it'll be about twelve degrees in here."

"I'm sure I'll be fine if you have lots of blankets."

Leah shrugged. "Suit yourself. I've got a down

sleeping bag and I'll throw a couple blankets over the clothesline. You can get them when you're ready to go to sleep."

Jackie looked around the living room. It was finished with a high-gloss pine and comprised the main area of the cabin, with the loft overhead, kitchen door on one side and a short hallway to the bathroom on the other. If there was only one bedroom, up in the loft, what did the doors across from the bathroom lead to? Two rooms was a lot of storage. She meandered over to the shelves, which were jammed with books.

"Help yourself to anything you'd like," Leah said. She closed the stove door and stood up.

"You're a mystery buff." Every detective she'd ever heard of was represented in the collection, along with names she didn't recognize.

"Not really."

Jackie knew when someone didn't want to talk about something. She had inherited a sense of diplomacy from her father. Her mother would have probed and ended up with Leah's life story — and Leah would have felt better for it. She changed the subject. "What used to hang here?" There was a subtle rectangular outline faded into the wood between the bookcases.

"A painting," Leah said. She took the tea kettle from the top of the Franklin stove and disappeared into the kitchen.

"Fine," Jackie muttered. Moody as her mother when she was working on a new piece. She settled down with a recent Brother Cadfael mystery. If silence was what her hostess wanted, silence was what she would get.

♥ ♥ ♥ ♥ ♥

As Leah filled the tea kettle, Butch rubbed her head against Leah's feet. She glared at the dog. Traitor, she thought. *You'll roll over for a pair of good hands and a pretty face.*

She was at a loss of what to say to Jackie. She wasn't the brainless teenager she'd first thought — definitely closer to thirty than twenty. She wanted to ask questions about Jellica Frakes, one of the few women in the arts Leah truly admired, but that would mean talking about who she was. And she didn't want to talk about herself or art. It hurt too much.

She went back to the spare room — Sharla had called it the dressing room — where all their clothes and the linens were stored, and brought out the sleeping bag and two blankets, a pair of Sharla's flannel PJs and thick cotton socks. She draped the blankets over the top of the clothes on the line. She hoped Jackie would be warm enough. Sharing her bed with another woman was not a welcome circumstance. Especially a woman that would be wearing Sharla's clothes.

She pled tiredness and left Jackie to enjoy the Bach and the book she'd become engrossed in. She changed into pajamas and climbed the ladder to the loft. To her surprise she found the sound of the music and turning pages comforting . . . sounds of life. It was a long time before she dozed off, but not as long as she had thought it would be.

* * *

Something woke her up. Not Butch moving around . . . she knew those noises. Something else. It was dark below, but the flickering flame from behind the glass in the Franklin stove gave some light. She sat up, saw someone moving around, then remembered her guest. It looked like she'd gotten up for another blanket from behind the stove. There was silence again and Leah went back to sleep.

The next time she woke she smelled something cooking. She sniffed. Soup? What was Sharla up to? She rolled over and blinked in the dim light coming from the skylight. And in the middle of the night?

"You know you don't want this carrot, so stop begging for it," she heard a voice say. Her blood froze. A wave of pain hit her so hard in the chest she collapsed back onto the bed barely able to breathe.

She's dead.

It was so easy to forget because she wanted to so badly. To pretend that the woman moving around in the kitchen was Sharla. But she wasn't.

For a long bitter moment, Leah wished she had left Jackie Frakes to freeze in the snow.

"You'll be sorry if I give you this. You don't like onion, you know that you don't." Another waft of something delicious found its way into the loft.

Leah wiped her eyes and looked at the clock. Just after eight . . . she wasn't used to getting up this early. In the winter she was early to bed and late to rise. It wasn't as though she had a reason to get up. It wasn't as though she could paint.

Today she had to get up to find out what this stranger was doing to her kitchen. She forced herself out of bed and threw on a robe. To her surprise, the fire in the living room was going quite nicely. From the heat flowing out of the kitchen, she guessed that Jackie Frakes had figured out how to stoke up the stove.

She headed to the bathroom without speaking. After her shower she glared at her reflection, aware that she looked at least five years older than her thirty-seven years. She started to put on her usual jeans and flannel shirt. She sighed and found clean black slacks and a sweater. Company.

When she finally went into the kitchen, she found Butch watching Jackie's every move with rapt attention. A pot boiling on the stove was the source of the soup smell. The turkey sat in a roasting pan. Jackie was dumping chopped celery and onion into a large bowl.

"Good morning," Jackie said. Much to Leah's relief, she was wearing her own clothes again. "I was going to make coffee, but I wasn't sure how you liked it . . . morning coffee is such a personal thing. I noticed you had a variety of beans."

Leah smiled slightly and busied herself with the coffee maker. She liked a mix of French roast and something flavored in the morning. This morning she felt like a dash of mocha almond. Thank God for Peet's mail order.

After a minute Jackie said, "Happy Thanksgiving,

by the way. I've got the giblets and neck boiling with some celery and carrot tops and onion. I chopped some celery and onion for the stuffing, but then I saw that you had bought apples and walnuts and I thought perhaps *they* were meant for the stuffing."

Leah stared at her. What a whirlwind of activity.

"You did want to have the turkey today, didn't you?"

"Yeah, I'm sorry. You've done a lot. Um, no apples for me in the stuffing, unless you want some . . ."

"I think it's vile."

Leah laughed. She hadn't meant to. "So do I. I like a plain celery and onion stuffing with reasonable seasonings. The apples and walnuts are for separate consumption."

"My mother went through a prolonged Indian cuisine stage, so we had apple and curry stuffing one year. With raisins. Never again." While she spoke, Jackie opened the bag of bread crumbs and dumped them in with the chopped vegetables. She added some melted butter and more of the boiling stock. Leah's stomach growled. She'd forgotten that Thanksgiving food smelled so good. She couldn't recall feeling this hungry in months.

Jackie continued, "It's not that I don't like Indian food. I love it. Give me a good curry, chapati and chutney, and I'll follow you anywhere." She finished stirring the mixture and began shoveling stuffing into the turkey. "In fact, Indian stuffing is really good if it's what you're expecting to come out of the turkey. But if you're not expecting it, it's quite disgusting."

"I know what you mean." Leah watched as Jackie rubbed the bird with buttered hands.

"Do you mind if I cook the bird my way? It'll turn out," Jackie said. She rinsed her hands and then tented the roaster with foil. "It's great to have a full kitchen at my disposal. My studio apartment doesn't have an oven and there's only two burners."

"The oven's too hot, isn't it?" Both dampers were wide open.

"Twenty-five minutes in four-fifty to five hundred degrees, then we turn it down to about three twenty-five. It'll sear the outer skin." Leah hurried to open the door when Jackie hoisted the roaster off the counter.

"Well, you've taken care of dinner, so let me make breakfast. How hungry are you?"

"Starved."

Newly aware that her guest might have exacting standards about food, Leah took care over the eggs and hashed potatoes. Jackie ate with relish and appreciation. Sharla had always been dieting. Leah shook her head to get the image of Sharla out of it.

"The phone's still dead. Do you think my uncle will come for me today?"

Leah glanced out the window where the snow was still coming down. "I really doubt it. Visibility's bad. And the snow's probably four to five feet at the bottom of the hills. It would be foolish. They won't plow up here till it stops snowing and then only after the main roads are cleared."

"How long will it last?"

Leah shrugged. "Looks like all day to me. Sorry."

"No, I'm the one who's sorry. You hardly expected a visitor, let alone one that stayed for days."

Leah was surprised that she smiled. "It's okay. My social skills were getting rusty."

"Look, I'm dying of curiosity about something," Jackie said. She gathered the breakfast dishes and headed for the sink. "How do you know my mother's work and why was there a box of costly art supplies sitting in the snow outside? I put in on the back porch, by the way."

Leah bit her lower lip. She was going to spend the whole day with this woman. It wasn't as though she could go for a long walk. "I'm an artist."

"Oh. That explains it." Jackie started to rinse the dishes and Leah felt a little let down. Then she realized that Jackie had probably met a lot of artists and aspiring artists. She permitted herself a moment of ego . . . she would have thought that Jellica Frakes's daughter would know her name.

Jackie was already a step ahead of her. "Leah Beck. Lee Beck. *Pieces of Eight*? *Many-Splendored Black and Red*? Are you *the* Lee Beck?"

Leah nodded. She watched the expressions flicker over Jackie's face. Jackie's cheekbones cast shadows into the hollows above her jaws . . . an interesting face, Leah thought. Not pretty, but very interesting. And the thick braid of deep brown hair that fell the length of her back plus a few inches — it was beautiful against the white of her sweater, even if it looked a bit scraggly after having been slept on.

She realized that Jackie was probably recalling everything she knew about Lee Beck. A widening of deep blue eyes . . . possibly she was recalling that Leah told the NEA to shove their grant. Thick, dark lashes flickered with something not quite fear, but surprise. Oh great, Leah thought. She just remembered I'm a lesbian.

Then the inevitable looking away. She's just

remembered Sharla died. Beautiful Sharla, the love of my life. She's going to say —

"I'm sorry," Jackie said.

"What for?"

"I don't think you wanted me to know." She turned back to the dishes. "I can see it calls up painful memories for you."

"I can handle it." Hah.

"That's why you left the art supplies outside."

Leah could tell that Jackie thought she was being self-indulgent. Stung, she said, "What the hell do you know about it?"

Jackie turned back from the suds in the sink. "You're not working."

Leah came up out of her chair. She could not believe this woman's insensitivity! "My negligence cost me the woman I loved. Excuse me for grieving. You don't know anything about it."

"I'm sorry. You're right, I don't," Jackie said. She turned back to the sink. "How frugal do I need to be with the hot water?"

Leah's mouth hung open for a moment. Of all the nerve, and then changing the subject. "The propane tank is near full and the hot water heater runs off that."

"Oh good," Jackie said. She ran more hot water into the sink.

Butch sidled up to Jackie's thighs, nudging none too gently. Traitor dog, Leah thought grimly.

Jackie glanced over her shoulder at Butch. "You should eat more than I've already given you? I'm not the person to beg from, you know." Butch whined, then padded over to nudge at Leah's fingers. Leah had half a mind to let her starve.

"What's she had?"

"She gummed a piece of carrot, then rejected it in favor of the rest of the can of Science Diet that was on the back porch. I let her out for a few minutes and when she came back in I fished a piece of boiled turkey meat out of the stock and she seemed to like that a lot when it cooled off."

"I'll bet she did. Time for some dry food, girl." Leah went out on the back porch and busied herself dishing out a good portion of dry food. Butch was a big dog. She then decided it was time to sweep out the porch — the dust was pretty thick in places. Who cared if it was a snow storm? She'd rather be out here than making small talk. Jackie didn't understand about grief, that much was abundantly clear — she was a *tabula rasa* when it came to pain.

She worked the broom into all the corners, disturbing dust that had been there when she and Sharla had bought the cabin eight years ago. Jackie Frakes didn't know what she was talking about. It had only been 25 months. You don't recover losing someone that fast, not someone she'd loved the way she'd loved Sharla. She could close her eyes and see Sharla crunching across the snow toward her. Sharla in all her elegance, her hair the color of maple leaves turning in the autumn.

Leah drew in a deep breath and swayed on her feet. Skin nearly translucent, skin that bruised from Leah's kisses in the wildest moments of their lovemaking. God, the sex — Sharla had been Leah's first and only lover, but Leah knew the love they'd made had been world-class. Sex too vivid for color, too tender for form.

Leah shuddered and opened her eyes. Snow swirled against the door to the back porch. She could hardly see the nearest tree let alone the meadow where Sharla had once danced and laughed. Self-indulgent? Was missing her, longing for her, remembering her self-indulgent?

The bang of a pot on the floor followed by low-voiced cursing snapped Leah back to what she had been doing. She looked down at the small pile. Too prosaic for her mood. She swept it into a dustpan, dumped it in the bin and went to see if she could lend Jackie a hand.

4

Jackie ladled gravy generously over her stuffing. She would need a nap after this, but if she said so herself, the meal had turned out wonderfully.

"It's not all that glamorous," Jackie said, in response to Leah's question. "My folks kept me out of the limelight. I was just another diplomatic corps brat, really. I didn't go the fancy dinners or meet heads of state. Well, I did meet and curtsey to Queen Elizabeth when I was eleven."

"What kind of life is it, though? Where did you

live?" Leah was dividing her attention between the turkey and the baked yams.

"Depending on the country, we lived in the city nearby or at the embassy. My mom was much happier when we lived in the cities. We lived in Oslo and The Hague. And Madrid. But we lived in the embassy anywhere south of that. I didn't get to see much of the African or Middle Eastern countries. My mom went outside more than I did. And I went to boarding school after I turned twelve."

"Where do you call home?"

Jackie swallowed a delectable mouthful of turkey and gravy. "San Francisco. I always wanted to live there. I have dual Canadian and U.S. citizenship, so I guess if I didn't love the Bay Area, I'd go for Vancouver or Victoria. When I'm a licensed architect it'll really depend on where the work is. At least the work I want to do." She made a face.

"I take it you're less than happy where you are."

"I could really hate it if I let myself. But I've got no one to blame but me. At least I can blame the car on Parker." She smiled wryly.

Leah paused in cutting another bite of turkey. "Let me get this straight about the car. You decided together that it made sense for *you* to buy a car so you could drive down to see him, and then *he* picked out the car?"

"That's not quite the way it happened," Jackie said. Put like that, it sounded like Parker was a chauvinist or something. He was in fact very sensitive to women's issues and she sought to defend him. "It was only when we were out looking and we found the MG —"

33

"But it wasn't the car you wanted and you were the one who was going to pay for it and drive it, right?"

She nodded.

"Well," Leah said. "Whatever."

Jackie let the silence grow. She supposed that her relationship with Parker wasn't something she could expect Leah to empathize with. She ignored the little voice that reminded her that she'd agreed to spend Thanksgiving with her aunt to make a break from the routine of seeing Parker every weekend.

"Why doesn't he drive up to see you?"

"His car has just enough life to get him to the office and back. And he works long hours."

"Longer than yours?"

Jackie nodded. "I generally work through about noon on Saturday, and he works until four or so. He's on contract, so he can come and go as he pleases, but he's on a very rigid production schedule. Software design is pretty complicated."

Leah snorted. "Lots more complicated than designing the requirements for a block of condominiums."

Jackie smiled. "Okay, architecture is complicated too."

Leah swallowed another mouthful of green beans, then said, "Well, I'm glad to see he supports you in your career."

Jackie decided the diplomatic thing to do was to take Leah's sarcasm at face value. "He does. I just wish he supported me in my choice of cars."

Leah cracked a smile. "Okay, I'll get off my feminist high horse for a while."

Jackie wrinkled her nose. "I'll be honest, it

34

bothers me. Considering that I could have frozen to death, it bothers me a lot. Our relationship's not perfect, but I've got almost three years in on his training."

"I thought you said you'd just moved here last year."

Jackie could feel herself flushing slightly. She hoped Leah thought it was the steam coming off the baked yams. "I did, but we met in Boston. I had finished my Master's and was working on my license. I need at least two years practical experience under another licensed architect."

"Umm-hmm," Leah said around a mouthful of stuffing and gravy.

"Parker was working for Lotus when he got this offer to consult in Silicon Valley."

Leah swallowed. "You were able to transfer out here in the middle of your certification?"

Jackie grimaced. "Yeah, but I had to give up a couple of months credit. California's requirements on experience credits were a little different. And the firm I'm with now is not as . . . interested in what I want to do. Their forte is large-scale commercial buildings. It was a change."

"From what?"

"From school. I went to Taliesin." Jackie felt herself flushing again. She knew what Leah was going to say. She was going to say exactly what her mother had said. Exactly what her father had said, though he had been extremely diplomatic about it.

"Let me get this straight." Leah leaned forward on her elbow and pointed at Jackie with her fork. "You went to the Frank Lloyd Wright School of Architecture. They have what — seventy-five, a hundred students a year?" Jackie nodded. "And just because what's-his-name wanted to take a job across the country you gave up your apprenticeship at the firm they placed you in?"

Jackie nodded.

"Couldn't he have waited and taken another job when you were through?"

Actually, Parker's not taking the job had never been discussed. Jackie wasn't about to admit that to Leah. "I didn't want to live apart."

"No regrets?"

"*Je ne regrette rien,*" Jackie said. "No regrets." But even to herself she didn't sound very convincing.

Leah pushed her plate away. "I'm stuffed. I need to walk this off."

"Still snowing," Jackie said. "But it's thinned out."

"Thanks for the great meal," Leah said. The gravy had made her tongue do flip flops. She had made a pig of herself and it had felt . . . good.

"Thanks for hauling me out of the snow." Jackie smiled and Leah couldn't stop herself from smiling back. "Why don't we clean up the mess I've made?"

"One last thing," Leah said. She looked down at Butch who had not moved from her side throughout the meal. "Don't get used to this, girl," she said as she set her plate down on the floor.

It took Butch five seconds to clean it, including a small dab of yams. She looked up, eager for more.

Jackie laughed and set her plate on the floor. After cleaning Jackie's plate Butch correctly surmised nothing more would be forthcoming, so she wandered into the living room.

Leah dried the dishes as Jackie handed them over. They were finishing up when Leah saw a light gleaming down through the kitchen window. "What's that?" She lifted the blinds to peek.

"The moon," Jackie said breathlessly. "There's a break in the storm."

They wrapped themselves in their jackets and went out on the front porch. With a bark of delight, Butch launched herself up the slope, disappearing from sight as she sank into the fresh powder. With a yelp she leapt out of the hole she'd made and into a new one and on up the hill.

Jackie clambered after Butch and Leah followed. They'd be wet through in a few minutes, but after being cramped inside all day it felt good to be out in the bracing cold. For a few minutes at least.

With a hoot, Jackie threw herself on her back into the snow. "Oh, this feels great! Like feathers! Perfect powder!" She clambered to her feet again, a dusting of snow over her hair and face. She threw herself in another direction. "God! I've been inside offices for too long. The air is like wine." She hooted with delight and spun in the snow like a child.

Leah stood frozen, her fingers itching. The top of her head felt as though it was burning. The moon hung low in the sky, casting a faint blue over the snow, across the ground, on the tips of the dark pines. Jackie was etched in cerulean. Her braid spun in the light, and her face reflected the moon's glow. Her cheekbones were dusted in *bleu céleste,* and her chin was a blur as she threw herself into another drift of the silver-blue snow.

Leah whirled and stumbled back to the house, and then into her studio. She shoved some blank canvases out of the way. Chalks, sketchpad. She rushed back to the porch, out into the snow, then onto her knees.

Jackie had stopped her playful attack on the snow and looked at Leah in concern.

"Keep playing," Leah said. "Ignore me."

Jackie started to say something, but then just smiled. With another shout of glee, she launched herself yet again into a snow drift.

She was a mosaic of blues and whites. Silvers edged around her skin. The brilliant amethyst of her jacket framed the planes and curves of her figure.

She played for several more minutes, throwing snowballs at Butch, who barked and tried to catch them, then refused to jump at more. They sank into the snow, breathing hard. The moonlight abruptly winked out.

"Well, that's the end of that." Jackie's voice floated down to Leah on the whisper of the breeze. "It's snowing again."

So it was. Wispy snowflakes floated down like tiny handkerchiefs. She stood up, feeling dizzy. Her knees ached with cold.

"You okay?"

"I was concentrating too hard, I guess. I'm fine."

"Let me give you a hand," Jackie said, reaching for Leah's arm.

Butch exploded out of the snow, her bulk throwing Jackie, Leah, the sketchpad and pencils in different directions. The sketchpad landed closest to Jackie. She snatched it up out of the wet.

Jackie was looking at the topmost picture. "It's

okay." She carried it carefully into the light of the porch. "This is beautiful." Leah reached for the sketchpad, but Jackie ignored her. She was staring at the drawing, then up the hill. "Yes, yes, it does look like that. The moonlight is both hot and cold."

Butch shook her coat free of snow, showering them with pellets of melting ice.

"Damn mutt," Leah swore. She was intensely uncomfortable with anyone looking at the first work she'd produced in more than two years. "She's probably toasty warm under all the fur. C'mon, girl, outta the way. C'mon!" She kneed Butch in the side again, but Butch didn't budge. Leah glowered at her. "How would you look as a fur coat?"

"Come on, Butch," Jackie said. She led the way into the house.

Butch followed, her tongue hanging out a mile.

Leah rolled her eyes and followed them into the warm house.

♥ ♥ ♥ ♥ ♥

Yawning, Jackie settled in under her layers of blankets for the second night. Butch curled up in front of the sofa. The firelight from the Franklin stove played over the bare wall where the painting had once hung.

Over the muted crackle of the fire Jackie could just hear sounds of movement from the room at the end of the hall. With a stammering explanation that she wanted to work out the sketches, Leah had retired there several hours ago and nothing but the rustle of paper had been heard since. Jackie had amused herself with the rest of the mystery she'd started the previous night. She tried the phone again to see if service was back, but the line remained dead. She changed into pajamas and snuggled down into the sleeping bag with V.I. Warshawsky. Butch had been content to have a Milk-Bone and sleep after her affray with the snow.

The brief exercise had left Jackie far too tired. She *had* been spending too much time either in the office or in the car. She promised herself she'd get back on a routine of exercise as soon as possible.

She heard the sound of paper being torn from a pad. A strange creature, Leah Beck, a.k.a. Lee Beck. Jackie knew more of Leah's work from her own studies than from anything her mother said, though she recalled her mother's pleased admiration when Leah had told the National Endowment for the Arts that she'd accept their award only when they signed a pledge to end artistic censorship. Otherwise, they could shove it.

Thinking of her mother recalled the way her mother had sworn Jackie was ruining her life by giving up the apprenticeship she'd had in Boston. She grimaced. *I'm too young to start admitting my mother was right about anything.* Truth was, she hated her job now. She could barely stomach the cookie cutter approach to designing places where people lived and worked, cranking out buildings that hundreds of thousands would look at and forget seeing every day. This apprenticeship program was a mill for churning out specs and blueprints — very little hands-on experience with clients was available and only token opportunities to develop anything from scratch.

She was too much her father to fool herself about

her skills. She was no Frank Lloyd Wright. But every ounce of creativity she did have was being ground out of her at Ledcor & Bidwell. As her mother had said it would be.

She tried to turn her thoughts from this unprofitable path. She'd been down it too much lately. She tried to think of how she'd get more exercise. Perhaps she could get Parker to go dancing with her. She hadn't been in ages and she dearly loved it. But Parker didn't like it as much and complained that she outmatched him, which made it no fun for him.

It was only a tiny mental step from the box where she kept her unrequited desire to go dancing to the dumpster where she kept her growing resentments about her job . . . and about Parker. She was aware that her bitterness about the career setback spilled over onto Parker. She resented him his success. She resented his salary being five times hers and that after moving across the country they lived in separate cities and only saw each other on the weekends, and then only after she drove down to San Jose. Driving to see him in the car that cost a fortune to park in San Francisco a full block from her dark, tiny studio third-floor walk-up. She resented that his apartment, with two bedrooms and a modern kitchen, was in a complex with pool and jacuzzi and free parking — all of which cost him less than her rent. She had almost no savings to speak of, while his bank balance was skyrocketing. He could have afforded a new car without a second thought.

She was enough her mother to tell herself firmly that she'd made her bed and now she had not only to lie in it, but get a good night's rest. She snuggled down into the sofa cushions and thought about getting one of the warm blankets.

She probably wouldn't have resented him so much if when she wasn't there he missed her, but she had the feeling she could skip seeing him and he wouldn't care. He hadn't been upset about her absence over the holiday weekend. She'd felt guilty about asking, but then he hadn't seemed to care. And she'd certainly had more fun than in a long time — making a big meal and having someone appreciate it. She'd forgotten how much she missed cooking. Her roommate in Boston had had an appreciative appetite, too, like Leah's.

Funny, she hadn't thought about Kelly in ages. She wondered how she was doing, where she was working. She regretted that she and Kelly had grown apart — Kelly and Parker had been oil and water. After she had moved in with Parker, Kelly had just drifted away.

Parker. She hadn't wanted to do this — adding up all that she'd given up for the sake of their relationship. Her apprenticeship in Boston. Kelly's friendship. Some of her parents' respect for her good sense. If she was being brutally honest, she'd given up some of her own self-respect. And all for a rut that was making her crazy.

She put the book down, suddenly near tears. This taking stock had been inevitable. She'd been avoiding it, but now it was too late to stop. Her mother hadn't really had to persuade her too much to come up to her aunt's for Thanksgiving. She'd been eager to get away, have a bit of a holiday from her dark apartment and from Parker. They hadn't gone anywhere together in ages.

Every weekend was exactly like the one before. Get off work at noon on Saturdays, hop in the car with her overnight bag already packed. Stop for gas — her cost. Stop for the groceries she knew he wouldn't have remembered to get, including condoms — her cost. Let herself in at Parker's around three. Wait for him to get home. Go out to dinner — Dutch treat. Maybe go to a movie — Dutch treat. Go back to his place, have sex, be asleep by eleven. At least, he was asleep.

The last four weekends she hadn't been able to sleep, so she'd gone down to the jacuzzi. She'd struck up a running conversation with a nurse who came at that hour to work the knots out of her calves after her shift. If she was truthful with herself, she'd admit she looked forward more to talking about books, movies and politics in the jacuzzi than to seeing Parker. Parker talked mostly about software and his co-workers.

A board creaked on the other side of the room and she and Butch both started up.

"Sorry," Leah said. "I was trying to be quiet. I thought you were asleep."

Jackie had to clear her throat to be sure her voice wouldn't quaver. "I was just lying here thinking."

"Oh." Leah snapped on the light in the kitchen. "You want some hot chocolate?"

"Sure." Jackie sat up. Anything to stop thinking. Leah did have social skills, she thought with a little smile. She shrugged into the chenille robe Leah had lent her and padded out to the kitchen in her thick socks.

"Can I ask you a question?"

"Okay," Leah said. She poured milk into a saucepan, then looked up expectantly.

"Whose clothes are these? They're too big for you." Jackie pulled on the front of the pajamas which even she didn't fill out completely.

"They're Sharla's." Jackie could see the walls coming down in Leah's eyes.

"I thought so. Thank you for letting me wear them."

"Necessity is the mother and all that." Leah studiously measured out cocoa powder. "After my upbringing? I could hardly throw away good cloth."

"Where'd you grow up?" Jackie settled at the kitchen table and pulled her feet up onto the chair. She tucked the robe around them.

"Lancaster County, Pennsylvania. Mennonite country."

"Amish?"

"Amish who use machinery. Cars only come in black in those parts and the chrome is painted black too. Can't be too gaudy." Leah smiled ruefully.

Jackie thought of Leah's thick tempera and semi-precious metal canvases that she'd seen pictured in art journals. "Your early work was an answer to that, wasn't it?"

Leah laughed. Jackie couldn't believe it — a genuine laugh. "Are you psychoanalyzing me?"

"No, just guessing. After all, in *Many-Splendored Black and Red,* you painted over all except the edges of the silver with black. I'm just your average art student."

"And I know what garbage they teach at art school."

"My mother was appalled, too. She said that the curriculum has fallen off about twenty percent and the lack of teaching about non-Western Civilization arts is criminal."

"She's right. The more I know of your mother, the more I like her. Can I interest you in a dash of Kahlua in your cocoa?" Jackie nodded a yes. Leah poured the steaming cocoa into two mugs, doctored each from a small bottle of Kahlua, and brought them to the table.

"She's a good mother and still somehow very cool," Jackie said. She sipped her cocoa, the soothing chocolate warmth coating her throat. The Kahlua added a little burn and made her nose tingle. "It's hard to explain. She always knew when to be my mom, when to be an adult person I could proudly show off to friends, and when to be my friend. It was my dad's idea to name me after Jackson Pollack, though."

Leah's lips turned up with the closest thing to genuine amusement Jackie had seen so far. "Your parents sound like intriguing personalities."

"They are. My father is a wit and very charming. He taught me how to dance and walk a reception line without feeling like a robot. And if Mom hadn't been an artist she would have made a great therapist. As I get older I realize how hard both my parents worked to make a home for me that felt safe and secure, even in places where there was a lot of conflict."

"Were you ever in danger?"

Jackie shook her head. "Not that I knew. But

when my dad was transferred to Egypt in the early eighties, I was sent to boarding school. I worried about them a lot, though. Particularly my mom. She didn't like to be cooped up in an embassy — she'd go off to the local markets to sketch or take language lessons. And she loves to cook with local foods."

"That explains a lot." Leah sat up in her chair with an intrigued look. "I wondered about the rhythm of her work. It's not strictly Western. And the shapes of the figures and choices of stone — it's because she got inside the different places she lived."

"She couldn't help it. Even in the U.S. she goes to flea markets, wherever people are buying and selling. She says that's where people are the most real."

"And that series called *Wall Street*. It was chilling. I literally shivered when I saw it."

Jackie sipped her cooling cocoa and smiled fondly. "Proof in point. She spent a week at the Stock Exchange. Have you seen her *Weavers* series?"

Leah shook her head. "I haven't really been keeping up."

"She did three figures based on a textiles market. All female figures. The forms are somewhat indistinct, but their hands and the yarns are amazingly detailed. It's as warm as *Wall Street* was cold."

Leah looked pensive. "I suppose I should get out, but not . . . not right away. Um, listen. Is it okay if I sketch you in this light? It'll help with the detail on the other sketches — well, if I decide to take them to canvas."

Jackie blinked. "Sure. That's okay." She had been sketched a lot. Her mother liked to teach kids drawing and Jackie had often been called upon to be their live subject. Her mother insisted art was a universal language.

Leah returned with pencil and sketchpad. "Keep talking. You can move. Just keep the light on your face."

Jackie sipped her cocoa. The Kahlua had left her with a pleasant glow inside and a tendency to smile. Parker drifted to the dim recesses of her mind. "If the snow stays light do you think anyone will come for me tomorrow?"

Leah shrugged as her pencil scratched over the paper. "I'm going to guess probably not. They won't plow up here until after the highway's cleared, and they won't be starting that until tomorrow — if the snow breaks." She stopped talking to stare intently at her.

"Oh goodie." Jackie leaned back in the chair and crossed her ankles. It was unsettling to have Leah's piercing gaze focused on her. "That means I can play in the snow and have a real day off instead of making nice with relatives I haven't seen since I was a baby."

"Why'd you come up to see them? Turn a bit to the left."

"My mom made me." Jackie laughed. "I know, I'm a little big for that, but she's very good at guilt when she wants to be. My coming up here lets her off the hook for another ten years. They don't really get along. My mom's way too outrageous for them." Her other reason, time away from Parker, she kept to herself.

"I would have never said Jellica Frakes was outrageous. Cutting edge, yes."

"It all depends on your point of reference. To her

family, she's leading a completely bizarre life. To most artists I suppose she seems conservative."

"Lift your chin." Leah was leaning closer, the pencil moving across the paper at light speed. "For my parents, guilt was a way of life. Any form of aspiration, creativity or love that wasn't directed at salvation was a sin. No ifs, ands or buts. My father was an elder in the church."

"When did you leave home?"

"When I was eighteen. It was evident I had some artistic talent and they sent me to a Christian university near nowhere, New Mexico, to teach me how to be a nice, Christian artist. That's where I met Sharla."

Jackie decided there was something special about the way Leah said Sharla's name. It vibrated. The way *Jellica* vibrated when her father said it. "Love at first sight?"

Leah shook her head. "It took a while. But she was resourceful and determined. And she was determined never to go home again. Sharlotte Kinsey from Norman, Oklahoma. Can you imagine being from a place so off the beaten track that the main sight for miles is an oil field? Lancaster County is small but beautiful, full of life. The greens in the spring would actually hurt my eyes..." Leah's pencil paused for a moment and her eyes glazed. Then she shook her head and the pencil began moving again. "After a while she was determined that I would never go home either. So I didn't. Could you lean forward? Rest your elbows on the table."

"It must have been hard," Jackie said as she complied with Leah's request. Leah scooted her chair closer and scanned Jackie's brows and forehead. Jackie dropped her gaze, unable to stare back.

Leah was silent for a long time. She reached across the table, tracing the eraser end of her pencil along the laugh line that creased the left corner of Jackie's mouth. Jackie controlled a shiver. Leah's mouth had parted slightly and she felt as if Leah's gaze was burning her lips.

Leah sat back suddenly and made a last addition to her sketch. She flipped the pad closed. "No," she said softly. "It wasn't hard. She made everything easy. For thirteen years everything was very easy. Only the last few have been a bitch." Leah got up abruptly and took her mug to the sink. "I think I'll turn in. Are you sure you're warm enough?"

Jackie raised her mug in salute. She was devoutly grateful the sketching session was over. "I am now. Thanks. The Kahlua was nice." Truth be told, she was sweating slightly. She grabbed a toasty warm blanket from the clothesline and tucked herself into the sleeping bag. Leah clambered up the ladder out of sight. After a few minutes, all was quiet.

Except for the rapid beating of Jackie's heart.

5

A feathery snow persisted until noon on Saturday. Jackie tried to earn her keep by shoveling most of the huge drift against the garage door to one side. Butch kept her company. The weather report said that the snow would continue in higher elevations — what's higher than here, she wondered — through the day, but that the sun would be out tomorrow. Towards sunset she thought she heard the faint echo of a snowplow hard at work, but it sounded a mountain or two away.

Leah helped shovel for a while but at Jackie's urging went back to her sketches. She seemed grateful for the turkey sandwich Jackie forced on her in the early afternoon. Refreshingly worn out with physical labor, Jackie turned her attention to stripping the turkey carcass and making soup stock, all the while not thinking about Parker. After that she made soup. And baking powder biscuits. The door to Leah's studio remained closed.

Long after sundown, Jackie finally knocked and carried in a steaming bowl of soup and some biscuits. Leah was dishevelled and drawn, and she murmured in a distracted way Jackie knew all too well from her mother's fits of artistic passion. She stoked up the fire in the pellet stove that heated the studio and left again, not even sure Leah had noticed her.

An hour later Leah emerged, bringing her dirty dishes. She held out the bowl like an adult Oliver Twist. "May I have s'more, sir?"

Jackie looked up from her novel and nodded at the pot on the corner of the stove. "It's still hot. Biscuits are wrapped in the tea towel in the basket." She sat up and stretched her spine. The kitchen chairs weren't that comfortable, but the heat from the stove was too blissful to leave.

"I had no idea my kitchen could turn out something so tasty. And the biscuits are good."

"There were a number of spices shoved in the back of that cabinet." Jackie pointed. "Plus some things that had changed organic states. I tossed them into the composter."

Leah shrugged as she sat down at the table. "I hope Parker appreciates you." She dunked a piece of biscuit into her soup. "At this point, anyone else's cooking seems like manna to me, but even so, this is extra good."

"The key to a successful Thanksgiving is using everything up. You now have several gallons of turkey stock. Butch, by the way, tells me she likes warm turkey stock on her kibble when it's cold."

Leah made a derisive noise. "Yeah, right." Butch didn't even raise her head. She looked like a worn out, pleased dog. "I'll bet she said she should get turkey every day."

Jackie laughed. "She's not that greedy. Once a week would do."

Leah got up for a second biscuit. With her back turned she said, "You didn't say if Parker appreciated you. Does he appreciate your culinary prowess? Everything you do for him?"

Jackie was slow to answer. Honesty seemed important at that moment. "It's not perfect, but I care a lot about him. He doesn't talk about his feelings easily." With a start, she realized she wasn't sure he had feelings to talk about.

Leah was shaking her head as she sat down again. "Care? Caring is not worth wasting your time over. When you *love* someone, it invades every part of your life." She closed her eyes and idly stirred her soup. "It's not something you can describe, it just is. Every breath is a part of your love. There are no colors for it but it's every color, too."

"You're describing obsession."

Leah pushed the bowl away as though she'd lost her appetite. "Who says where it goes over the line? Love *is* obsession. Every little thing about her is beautiful, even the little things you can't stand. You want to know her thoughts and how she spends her time away from you. And she shares them with you because she feels the same way. That's not obsession, not when she loves you back. Not when she's obsessed with you too."

Leah wasn't speaking to Jackie, she was speaking to the blank wall that bore the outline of a canvas. Jackie didn't agree with Leah's definition of love . . . it wasn't anything like what she felt for Parker.

"People don't want to admit to that kind of love. Because if you can feel it, you can feel pain, too. The kind of pain that cripples your spirit." Leah bit her lower lip. "If only . . ."

In the golden light of the kitchen lamps, Jackie could see the glimmer of tears reflected in Leah's eyes. With a part of her that had nothing to do with her eyes, Jackie could see the black aura hanging around Leah, a pall of sorrow and hopelessness. It sent a chill up her spine and dusted her arms with gooseflesh.

She didn't know why she pressed Leah for more. "If only?"

"If only I had checked the lines myself instead of leaving it to the rental crew. The weather report was good for sailing, but the wind blew up unexpectedly. If only I'd headed in then. If only I'd made sure she'd tied her life jacket on tight. The mast snapped," Leah said with half-gasp. "Like a toothpick. And we capsized. I saw her head hit the railing as she went over. I couldn't reach her. She just slipped away from me."

A tear spilled over and shimmered like a diamond on Leah's hollow cheek. "It was like watching a leaf wash down a flooded river. Her face, then her hair, then just her fingertips. Her life jacket slid off of her and then she was gone." On the last word, Leah ran out of breath. Jackie could see her fighting to breathe in. When she finally did, it was a long, racking sob that drew Jackie out of her chair to Leah's side.

Without hesitation, she pulled Leah into her arms, cradling her head against her breasts. Leah pushed against her for a moment, then relented. From between them Jackie heard her say, "Her body washed up in San Pablo Bay two days later. Her family claimed it. They wouldn't let me go to the funeral. They took her body away and I never got to say goodbye."

"They shouldn't have kept you away," Jackie said. Leah's body was shuddering.

Leah pushed her away. "Where was their fucking Christian charity?" She gripped Jackie's arms with her powerful hands and stared up at her with eyes like hot irons. "If God is love and Jesus is their friend, then why wouldn't they tell me where the funeral was? Why wouldn't they tell me where she's buried?"

Jackie winced as Leah squeezed her arms. "I don't know, Leah. They were wrong."

Leah shoved her away and leapt up from her chair. She scrambled up the ladder to the loft without a backward glance, leaving Jackie to rub her bruised arms and stare up at the dark loft.

She had a lump in her throat. If something happened to Parker, would she feel that much anguish and grief? Two years or more later? No, she told herself. The answer was no. And she was a fool to continue thinking otherwise and to continue sacrificing for the sake of their relationship. She didn't feel for him or from him what her parents felt for each other. She didn't feel what Leah had obviously felt for Sharla.

That they were lesbians didn't trouble her. Both her parents had taught her that people's private lives were their own and it wasn't her place to judge them. She herself didn't have sexual feelings about other women, but that didn't mean what they felt for each other was any less real. She understood it on an intellectual level. She turned away from that thought, though it troubled her somehow, and not intellectually. She did not want to think about Leah with Sharla.

As she poked listlessly at the fire in the living room stove, she dwelled on the subject of Parker. All her mother's pointed remarks to the contrary, it hadn't been until Leah had asked if Parker appreciated her that she'd realized what her mother had been trying to tell her. Parker didn't value her as much as she valued him. She hadn't quite realized how accommodating she had been to maintain their relationship.

The more she thought about the car the more it pissed her off. Just because Parker made more by the hour didn't mean his leisure time was more valuable than hers. Why was she always the one to go to him? And because she did all the commuting, she'd hardly had a moment to explore San Francisco. Never driven up to the Muir Redwoods, for example, a mere 30 minutes away. Or driven through Wine Country in the summer, or down to Monterey in the fall — both were no more than three hours away from San Francisco.

She unbraided her hair and slowly brushed out the snarls, all the while asking herself what she got in return from Parker for her devotion, her sacrifice and her steadfastness. What did he give of himself for their relationship? Including gas, groceries, movie, dinner, tax and tip, every weekend she went to see him cost her almost half of her net pay for the week. It wasn't that she was putting a price on seeing him — oh hell, maybe she was. It just seemed like it wasn't worth it. She got nothing in return.

She couldn't think of anything. Not one single thing. Just last weekend Marge, the nurse she'd been meeting up with in the jacuzzi, had brought along an extra couple of cookies on the off-chance that Jackie would be there. Her kind gesture was more than Parker ever managed. He'd even stopped keeping her favorite soft drink in the house. If she wanted some she had to bring it — and pay for it — herself.

She drifted to sleep without intending to and woke some time later because she was freezing. The living room fire had gone out. Her fault — she hadn't been concentrating on stoking it up before she went to sleep.

She warmed herself next to the banked kitchen stove, but it wasn't enough, even wrapped in a blanket. And she couldn't sleep on the kitchen floor — it would leach all the heat out of her body.

She looked at the ladder to the loft and shuddered violently from the cold. Maybe Leah wouldn't like it, but she had to sleep up there. Leah had said it was a king, so she should be able to slip in without disturbing her.

She moved as quietly as possible up the ladder, no easy feat since she was shivering from head to toe. She heard the steady sound of Leah's breathing. The temperature was almost bearable when she reached the loft floor. Her eyes were adjusted enough to the dark to see that Leah was on the near side of the bed, so she carefully stepped around to the far side.

She saw the dim glow of an electric blanket light, so she stripped down to her T-shirt and panties, then slipped between the sheets. Leah's breathing remained steady and deep. The warmth eased her shivers almost immediately, spreading a sensual relaxation through her fingertips and toes. In minutes she was asleep.

♥ ♥ ♥ ♥ ♥

Leah was having a beautiful dream and she hoped it wouldn't end soon. Under her hand was soft stomach. She moved slowly, trying to keep the spell. Fine ribs under her fingertips.

It had been so long since her fingertips had felt this alive.

She ran her fingers over the velvet skin and in her dream heard a soft sigh and the rustle of bedclothes. The body was closer to her now. She could stroke the smooth back.

It wasn't Sharla's back. That's what she would have expected in a dream, but this back felt different. *I still love you, my darling.* But she would give herself this dream because it felt good.

Her own body felt ripe and heavy as she caressed the dream woman. She felt a little dizzy because her fingertips were sending her such vivid, tactile sensations. She moved closer very slowly, afraid of

waking herself. Finally from out of a tousle of hair —
too much hair to be Sharla — she could see a
sensuous column of throat. She moved the silky
brown strands aside and pressed her lips to the
pulse.

The fire in her limbs leapt to full height. She
kissed the throat, then the shoulders, again and again
and knew she would wake herself, but she couldn't
stop as her need burned stronger with each kiss.

Then the dream woman sighed — a soft oh and a
deep breath. She moved into Leah's arms and Leah
couldn't restrain herself. Her hands caressed the
melting breasts, then she took one in her mouth. The
dream woman quivered in her arms and her back
arched, offering.

They moaned together.

Leah jerked herself away just as Jackie went rigid
and gasped, "No."

"I'm sorry," Leah gasped back. In the dim light
she could see Jackie frantically pulling her T-shirt
down, yanking the covers up over her shoulders,
putting barriers up between them. Leah said more
calmly, "I didn't know what I was doing. I thought
you were a dream."

Jackie said, "It's okay. I understand. I should
have stayed downstairs, but the fire went out. I'm
sorry. I didn't mean —"

"Of course not. I didn't either —"

"I was surprised, that's all —"

"It's okay. I started it. I thought you were Sharla.
I was dreaming." That was a lie, Leah knew.

Jackie said again, "It's okay. I was just
surprised."

And you were enjoying it, Leah thought. Until

58

you were fully aware it was me, you were responding. *Oh lay off it.* She told herself crossly that even if deep down they were all sexual animals it didn't mean that Jackie was on the verge of becoming a lesbian. *She was probably dreaming about her boyfriend and one pair of hands is much like another. Sooner or later she would miss that all-important thing men've got.*

"I promise to stay on my side," she said aloud. "I didn't know you were there. There won't be any repeats."

"I trust you," Jackie said quietly in the dark. "It's okay. Let's go back to sleep."

Leah curled into a motionless ball. She felt miserable and told herself it was because she had betrayed her memory of Sharla. She told herself that she could sleep, despite the needles of sensation that reminded her that she was a living woman with a real, live libido and that Sharla — her loving, compassionate Sharla — would have understood.

Jackie emerged from the shower wrapped tightly in Sharla's chenille robe. Her hair hung in a curtain down her back and Leah's fingers twitched as she recalled too vividly what it had felt like last night. She was aware that Jackie wouldn't meet her gaze. She herself was too aware of how she had wanted that body — not Sharla's, not any woman's, but Jackie's body — near her. No matter how often she reminded herself that Jackie had a boyfriend waiting for her, the prickling in her fingers wouldn't go away.

"I'll make eggs," was all she said. "As a break from turkey leftovers."

"Sounds good."

Leah gathered the ingredients from the fridge, staring intently at the egg carton to avoid any eye contact with Jackie.

As she set them down, Jackie said hesitantly, "Before you start that, I just need to clear the air about last night."

"It's okay," Leah said. "I really don't know why I stepped over the line like that."

"I don't know why I did either," Jackie said.

Her voice was low and Leah heard her swallow. She turned to look at her, to watch that face flicker with emotions. She would paint it gray uncertainty, purple determination, chartreuse fear.

"I have to be honest with you," Jackie continued. "I — I've never wanted a woman before. But I knew . . . last night. That you were a woman. I know I said stop, but that was the surprise of it. I didn't want you to stop. And now —" She put one hand to her throat and swallowed again. "I'm not sure what to do about it."

Leah shook her head, deeply sorry about the mess she'd gotten them into. No matter what her own body wanted, she had to be firm. "I don't . . . I don't help straight women assuage their curiosity. You'll have to find someone else." Leah found herself swallowing hard, too. She felt short of breath.

"That's not — I'm sorry, I didn't realize what I was asking. What . . . oh shit." Jackie's face was flushing crimson. The patch of skin visible at the top of the robe was tinted orchid pink. "Forget I brought it up. I've made everything awkward."

"If you're really questioning —"

"I don't know!" Jackie looked down at her feet. "The way my body feels doesn't make any sense. It feels strange, different. But you're right, I can't just ask you to work this out for me. I have to do it myself."

Leah realized she *was* breathing hard. She had also unconsciously moved closer. "Jackie, it's not that I don't . . ." *Want you.* She did. Jackie had marched in here and dispelled Sharla's ghost. She wanted to hold onto this warm, breathing, lovely body as long as she could.

Jackie's gaze was unfocused, her mouth slightly parted. Leah couldn't stop herself from staring at Jackie's lips. She'd stared at them too long last night. She had wanted to touch them too much last night. They were even fuller than before, glistening. She devoured the rest of the face that she had already spent hours sketching. Skin flushed, slightly damp.

She pulled slowly and gently on the lapel of Sharla's robe. The knot around Jackie's waist loosened. Sharla's robe, but Jackie's body within.

She could see Jackie's nipples thrusting hard against the chenille, rising and falling as she gasped for breath. Leah tightened her grasp on the robe and the knot fell open. Leah's vision swam as she took in the plush, pliant swell of Jackie's stomach and the dark tangle of hair below it.

She heard Jackie's voice from far away. "God, Leah, I don't know what to do. But I want to do it."

Her hands slipped around Jackie's waist. She stepped into the widening circle of Jackie's arms. Jackie's lips were eager and welcoming when Leah kissed her.

With a moan Jackie drew Leah's body fully against her own. Leah wouldn't have pressed Jackie so hard against the counter, but Jackie was tightening her arms, crushing Leah's mouth with painful need. She murmured small noises of pleasure and invited Leah to explore her mouth with a breathless brush of her tongue against Leah's.

Leah revelled in the sweetness that waited for her. She thirsted for more. Her hands gripped Jackie's ribs, then, more roughly than she meant to, she grasped Jackie's breasts. Jackie broke the bruising hunger of their kiss.

"I'm sorry," Leah gasped. "I didn't mean to frighten you."

"I'm scared," Jackie whispered. "I'm scared to death." Her lips were trembling. Then she drew Leah's hands to her breasts again and shuddered as Leah stroked them. She was breathing hard and the arms she put around Leah's neck were shaking. But she pulled Leah's face down again for another kiss as Leah explored the fullness of Jackie's breasts.

Time passed in uneven waves until Leah raised her head at an unfamiliar sound. A car horn.

Jackie stiffened. The horn repeated again. A man's voice halloed down from the road. Jackie gave a cry of frustration and Leah realized Jackie was near tears.

"That must be your uncle," Leah managed to say. In the short pause they heard a door slam and the sound of the gate opening.

Jackie nodded mutely. Leah watched the planes and angles try to sort themselves into the order Leah had sketched yesterday, but her lips looked too kissed, her face too stricken.

Then she realized Jackie was leaving. *Leaving.*
The gate clanged shut and the sound was a punch in
the stomach.

She whispered, "You're going away with them."
What am I going to do, she thought desperately. I
can't ask her to stay. She can't leave, she can't!

"I don't want to go," Jackie said. "Not yet."

"You want to know what you're missing," Leah
said bitterly. "You want to know?" Jackie stared at
her, then didn't resist as Leah pulled her into her
arms for a harsh, hungry kiss.

"This is what you're missing," she whispered in
Jackie's ear. Her fingers slipped between Jackie's
thighs. Jackie pulled away slightly, then her legs
opened. Leah nearly cried out at the silken wetness
that greeted her. She thrust in, her fingers coated.

"Oh God," Jackie gasped. She threw her head
back, moaning. "Yes."

"This is what you're missing," Leah whispered
fiercely, looking into Jackie's face. "It's like this
between women. It's called fucking, Jackie." Jackie
groaned, her mouth open, eyes almost closed.
"There's more, so much more."

Steps sounded on the walk outside. Leah pushed
Jackie away, turned blindly to the sink. "Maybe when
you're with him you'll imagine my mouth on you and
wonder what it would have felt like."

Jackie let out a sound like a sob and ran from
the kitchen. Leah shoved her hands under the tap,
scrubbing away the traces of Jackie's readiness. She
met Jackie's uncle as he knocked on the door.

Somehow she greeted him civilly. They'd met at
the post office and market once or twice, and out
walking in the woods. He was always civil. She

invited him to warm up next to the fire while Jackie supposedly finished her shower. She asked about the height of the snow and pretended to listen to the detailed answer and his explanation of how they'd already winched Jackie's car up onto the road again. When Jackie hurried in, fully dressed in her own clothes, her face was as cool and calm as Leah had ever seen it. Glacier blue. Leah felt the familiar wall of unfeeling cold close around her.

She offered Jackie a pair of her gloves. Jackie insisted that Leah write out her address so she'd know where to send them.

They shook hands. Jackie's hand was like ice, but it trembled in Leah's grip.

Leah watched her trudge up the slope to her uncle's truck, then she pulled Butch out of the doorway and shut the door on the picture of Jackie going out of her life before she was really in it.

She'd been cruel. She'd never forgive herself.

Her own pain was almost too much to bear.

Butch began barking and wouldn't stop. Leah escaped into her studio and stared down at the sketches of the face she thought she'd known yesterday.

She seized a new pad. Any chalk, any color would do for now. Today's face slowly developed out of the paper like a photograph absorbing light. Jackie wanting her.

She tore the sheet from the pad and let it fall to the floor.

Jackie saying yes.

Colors this time.

The blue and silver of Jackie saying yes.

6

"If I didn't know better, I'd say you had the flu." Mary Nguyen leaned against Jackie's cubicle wall and regarded her with a faint hint of worry in her usually calm eyes.

Jackie had trouble meeting Mary's deep brown gaze. She'd been having trouble looking women in the face ever since the weekend. "How do you know I don't have the flu?"

"Because if you did you'd have called in sick like anyone with sense." She chewed on her lower lip.

"I'd trade a nice case of the flu for a week slaving on Mannings' behalf."

"Be careful what you wish for . . ." Jackie smiled weakly.

Mary shrugged. "I know, I could get it. When do you think the big powwow will be over?"

It was Jackie's turn to shrug. Ledcor & Bidwell's key partners were in conference with the representatives of a small but prominent nonprofit housing developer. "I don't know why they're so hot to have this project. It's too small for them."

"Politics, that's why. It may be small, but every city official will know the name of the architects who worked on it. And it's an affordable housing demonstration project that'll hopefully be repeated nationwide. The free publicity is worth a mint."

Jackie nodded. She knew all this. She'd been asked to submit a set of designs for review by the partners, but hers had not been chosen for the final presentation to the client. Small wonder. The overall concept she'd gone with was blending into the affluent neighborhood to look like just another small apartment building with classic lines. Her creative efforts had been spent on the interior. Jackie didn't think people who lived there would want the building to stand out so everyone could point and say, "That's where the low income people live." Nor did she think the more affluent residents of the block would take to the extra traffic a "showpiece" would create. She'd bet they were already upset enough about low income people moving in.

Well, what did she know about it? The drawings that were being presented had been drawn up by the general partner and featured a post-modern art deco exterior.

"So why do you look so blue? You've been like this all week."

Jackie realized she'd drifted off in the middle of her conversation. She'd been doing that ever since she'd left Leah's house. Left Leah's arms. *It's called fucking, Jackie.* She shuddered from head to toe. Leah's voice whispered in her ear constantly, despite her attempts to get Leah out of her head.

"Are you sure you're not sick?" Mary's eyes reflected sympathetic concern.

All at once, Jackie registered Mary's short, short hair and thin braid, and the demure but still noticeable gold ear cuff. Stop it, she told herself. Lots of women in San Francisco look like that and they can't *all* be lesbians. She realized she hadn't answered Mary. "Maybe I am. I've been feeling very . . . strange lately."

A new voice cut across their conversation. "Sorry to interrupt, gals." Mannings leaned into Jackie's cube. "Could you gather your drawings for the AH project and come with me?"

Mystified, Jackie did as he'd asked and followed Mannings to the conference room.

"I'm afraid they don't care for the designs we've shown them and they hinted they wanted something less flashy."

Jackie let sarcasm creep into her voice. "So you thought of me."

Mannings gave her his snake-oil smile. "I thought your designs very good but I couldn't very well gainsay Randall, now could I?"

As Jackie straightened her jacket, she felt a familiar swelling of distaste for Mannings and L&B in general, tempered with the knowledge that she was feeling peevish because it had been her choice and hers alone to come here. At least she wasn't thinking about Leah. At least not much. She hadn't sent the gloves back yet because she didn't know what to put in the note. *Thank you for turning my life upside down . . . thank you for making me want you . . .*

"This is Jackie Frakes, one of our associates," Randall announced after a nod of greeting in her direction. Jackie realized the general partner wasn't going to admit she wasn't yet licensed. "Jackie was tops in her class at Taliesin, a very exclusive architecture school. You have the designs we worked on, don't you Jackie?" He smiled benevolently at her.

She did her best to hide her disbelief. The designs we worked on, she wanted to echo. She swallowed her disbelief and patiently set her drawings out on the table facing the row of client representatives and then unrolled the preliminary blueprints.

A large, stately black woman immediately picked up one of the exterior sketches. "Yes, this is much more what I have in mind. The project blends in." She looked at Jackie appraisingly. "I'm B.J. Taylor, and your name again was?"

Gratified, Jackie told her and then went into her cost estimates in some detail. She could tell Ms. Taylor and the others were pleased with the efforts she'd put into building out the interior with an eye to lower maintenance and upkeep costs in the long run. She could also feel that Randall was glad to have the clients delve into the details so thoroughly.

The group got up to leave about forty-five minutes later. Speaking directly to Jackie, Ms. Taylor said, "I'm very impressed. Frankly, we've only seen work like this from one other firm. You've managed to make the inside dimensions unusual but completely functional. Just because the outside blends in doesn't mean the inside should be boring. I would say we'll be deciding between your concept and the one we saw earlier today." There were nods of agreement all around.

Jackie thanked her and rose to her feet to shake hands.

Mannings said, "I hope it's not too forward of me to ask who the other firm is?"

"Neighborhood Design and Aesthetics."

Jackie could tell Randall and Mannings were hiding grimaces of distaste. Obviously, neither thought Neighborhood Design was in L&B's league.

Jackie sat in a daze while Randall escorted the clients to the main door and then returned. He was the picture of geniality.

"I think once they see the depth of experience that L&B can offer NDA doesn't stand a chance." He jangled change in his pocket while Mannings made noises of agreement.

Jackie found her voice and tried very hard to sound reasonable but firm, the way her father did when his patience was tried. "I'm very uncomfortable with the impression the client has. They're under the impression that I'm licensed."

"As long as the drawings have my name on them there's no problem," Randall said. Jackie realized he saw nothing wrong with the arrangement. Was this business as usual, she wondered. "Of course they need some modification, which I'll do as I work with the client."

"I want to be sure I'm clear about this arrangement," Jackie said slowly. Her voice was threatening to quaver. "At this point you're going to take my work and I won't be working with the client at all."

"The client will expect to work with a partner," Mannings said. "And working with Randall himself will demonstrate that even though the project is small, we take it very seriously."

Jackie gave him The Look. She knew that her work belonged to L&B and they could do what they liked with it. She could even live with losing credit for it. But not to be allowed to work on the project as it took shape — it would be like a chef never tasting her own food. "I would still like to keep my hand in. The client will never know I did the design on my own," she said. She had tried to sound calm, but her tone was belligerent.

"You're in training. If you want credit for your time..." Randall's voice trailed away significantly.

Jackie straightened her spine. So she was questioning all the other aspects of her life — sex, love, commitment, everything. But she knew her own value at her work. She wasn't great, but she was very good. Her self-confidence was something they couldn't take. "Then I should not care that I won't even get to work on it?"

Randall said to Mannings, "I don't think that Taliesin does a good job of preparing students for the real world." He turned his back completely on her.

Jackie swallowed. Her stomach knotted. "Excuse

me, but I think I have the flu. I haven't been feeling like myself for the last few days." She turned on her heel and walked out, trying to look as dignified as her mother had when she'd walked out of an art exhibit she'd found distasteful. She stopped at her desk long enough to pick up her fanny pack, satchel and coat.

In the elevator to the street she realized she was probably going to get fired, which would mean starting over with another architect. Mannings might not even sign her work-experience certificate.

She shivered for most of the bus ride home. Somehow she had managed to appear lighthearted at her aunt's. The drive home had been a blur. She'd been feeling weepy all week and tears leaked out of the corners of her eyes. Lacking tissues, she used her sleeve to wipe away the trickles. She pushed back the sleeves for a moment and studied the bruises Leah had left on her arms after she'd cried for Sharla. They were fading, but they were the only thing about the weekend that was.

She stopped at the bakery on the corner and bought the largest, gooeyest cinnamon roll they had and then trudged up the three flights to her studio in the Victorian's attic. Its only good point was lack of next door neighbors. With the door locked behind her she allowed herself a self-indulgent cry.

When the tears abated she washed her face, took some aspirin and ate the cinnamon roll. She felt better with the sugar buzzing in her system. A creamy cup of her favorite blend of Peet's decaf — vanilla roast — restored some of her spirits.

When she had reached the stage of upbraiding herself for being a baby, the phone rang. She debated answering it. She decided she would — if it was Mannings she'd sound sniffling enough to convince him she really was sick.

Her mother's voice poured over the line and Jackie instantly felt better. Then she felt alarmed. "Why are you calling? Is Dad okay?"

"Yes, everything is fine, although you sound as if you have a cold. Is that why you're home? I called your office and they said you had left."

"No, just recovering from a crying jag. So what's up?"

"No, no, you first," her mother said. "Jackson, what's the matter? I knew I should call you today, I just knew it." The light voice sounded a good deal closer than the other side of the planet and it soothed Jackie's ragged nerves.

"I had a fight with the general partner. I think I'm going to get fired." She filled her mother in with every detail and felt gratified by her mother's supportive and righteous indignation. She didn't want to tell her mother — not yet — about the other problem. Leah's voice whispering, *It's like this between women . . .*

"Well, dear, it seems to me that the best way to avoid being fired is to find another job first."

"Where would I start?" Jackie stretched out on the sofa bed.

"How should I know? There's always the Yellow Pages."

"Wait, I know! I'll start with the firm the client mentioned today. Neighborhood Design and Aesthetics. Someone there thinks like me."

"A promising name for someone who won an

award for her community neighborhood plan, remember?"

"Yeah, thanks for reminding me I'm not a worthless slug." Jackie was smiling again.

"Better now?"

"Better. Thanks, Mom. Your intuition remains amazing."

"All in a day's work, Jacks."

"So why did you call?"

"I'm going to be in Dallas in the first part of January. I don't suppose there's any way you could fly in over the weekend? I'll arrange for your ticket. It'll make up for not being able to see you at Christmas. I'm so sorry about that."

"Don't beat yourself up about it. I understand Dad's commitments. But I'd love to see you in January, that would be great. It's about a three-hour flight from here, easy to do even if I don't have any time off. Of course, if I'm not working, I'll have all the time in the world." Something in her heart eased knowing she'd be able to see her mother face to face. She could talk to her about Leah.

"Tell you what. You make your flight arrangements as soon as you know what you can do. Take my American Express number. Charge the ticket to that." Jackie wrote it down. "I'll call you next Thursday and get your itinerary."

They talked for a few more minutes and Jackie felt enormously better after her mother had hung up. Her sinuses were almost normal again and her headache had faded away. She felt better than she had since the weekend — since Leah.

She groaned and rolled over. Why did she go on

remembering? She dreaded seeing Parker again. She was afraid that when he touched her she'd think of Leah. If not of Leah, then of women. She knew he wasn't the life partner she'd dreamed of finding. She was feeling sexual desires he'd never satisfy — that he'd never try to satisfy. *You'll imagine my mouth on you and wonder what it would have felt like.*

She wondered, oh how she wondered. Like she'd never wondered before. How could she know she wanted something she'd never had? And it wasn't just wanting it, it was wanting to do it. Her head filled over and over again with visions of Leah's kitchen. This time it was Leah with her back against the counter, Leah with her legs opening . . .

She covered her head with a pillow. Damn it, damn it, she thought. It would have been okay to realize she needed to break with Parker. That wouldn't have been nearly as hard as realizing she should reconsider her every assumption about passion, about sex, about what made her libido tick.

She tried to shut her eyes against thinking about how Leah had made her body feel, but it didn't work. It had been an enormous surge of passion, like nothing she had felt before — the thrill of creating new designs, skiing a challenging run of fresh powder, helicopter flights. They all paled in comparison to the way Leah's fingers had felt taking her.

She'd realized too late that she would have happily stayed with Leah. Forgotten about her job, her family. Stayed and made love. *You'll imagine my mouth on you . . .*

When she could think past the promise of passion, she could feel the pull of comfort. It had felt right to be in the company of a woman. The ease was something she hadn't felt since graduate school. She'd shared her living quarters with Kelly Baines for all three years. Neither of them had dated much — school hadn't left much energy. They'd studied together, worked in Taliesin's communal kitchens together and had called each other best friend. Or had it been more than that? With neither of them knowing enough to reach across the small gap between their beds in the winter, their cots in the summer.

Kelly and she had both taken apprenticeships in Boston but at different firms. Jackie had had another choice, but going to Boston with Kelly had been the only option she'd considered. When she started dating Parker, Kelly became distant. They'd never had a fight, but Kelly's simmering, unspoken resentment of Parker had pushed Jackie to agree to move in with him. When she'd met Kelly for coffee to tell her she was moving to California, Kelly hadn't seemed to care and nonetheless had seemed real pissed about it.

She threw the pillow across the room and sat up. This endless revisioning of everything she'd done in her entire life wasn't getting her anywhere. Her headache was coming back. She seized the phone book and looked up the phone number for Neighborhood Design and Aesthetics. It was just after six o'clock, but she knew if it was anything like every other architect's office she'd worked in, there would still be people working. At least she would find out who the G.P. was and could send a resumé properly addressed tomorrow.

A woman answered the phone with a brisk tone. Jackie asked for the name of the G.P.

"Angela Martine." The voice didn't quite snap, but

Jackie knew whoever it was on the line had better things to do with her time than answer general inquiries.

"Do you happen to know if she or another partner is looking for an architect in training?"

"Are you looking for a placement? Because we just lost someone."

"Yes, yes, I am. I'm currently with a firm, but I think I need to find another situation." Jackie stopped herself from spilling out the whole story. "I'm sorry, I don't mean to be wasting your time."

"Are you in your first or second year of credit?"

"Second, if you would accept the training I've done so far. My degree's from Taliesin."

There was a silence. Then the woman said, "Come and see me early tomorrow morning. Say seven-thirty?" She sounded as if she already regretted her impulse.

"I'll be there." Jackie tried to keep from sounding eager, but she couldn't help it.

"Who are you?"

"Jackie Frakes. Who should I ask for?"

"Me. Angela Martine."

Jackie stammered her thanks as she ended the call. She eagerly spent an hour putting together her portfolio, which boosted her self-esteem a bit. She zipped it closed, then went for a brisk walk to tire herself out. She would be poised and self-assured and needed a better night's rest than she'd had all week.

She did sleep, but only after she relived again the breathless moments with Leah in her kitchen. The way Leah had seemed to know how to touch her breasts. The way Leah's fingers had known . . .

You'll imagine my mouth on you . . .

♥ ♥ ♥ ♥ ♥

Angela Martine was in her mid-fifties with rich, black hair that grayed at the temples, forming a severe frame for a hawk-like nose. Her no-nonsense voice carried a faint accent — Mexican, maybe, Jackie thought. Angela briskly directed Jackie into her office. She felt some of her self-assurance slipping away as she sat down across the cluttered desk from Angela and was met with a frank stare. Aztec, that was it. Angela's profile could have come right off an Aztec sculpture.

"Before I spend any time looking at your portfolio, maybe you should tell me why you're looking for a change in jobs." Angela leaned back in her chair, her face unreadable.

"Well, for reasons I won't bore you with, I made a mistake in accepting a position with Ledcor and Bidwell. I should have stayed at the firm Taliesin had placed me in — Ellis and Ellis out of Boston. My situation at L&B is that I recently did a set of drawings for a small project which the client has ended up preferring. The G.P.'s name is on it and he isn't going to let me do any further work on the project even though during the presentation I thought I developed a good rapport with the client. The client was left with the impression that I was licensed and would be their contact — false pretenses, in my opinion." Jackie couldn't tell if Angela was shocked by that or was wondering why Jackie had been upset. "I would have been able to swallow the situation and finish my training except I . . . made another mistake in judgment." Jackie stopped for breath and Angela cut in.

"You let them know that it upset you."

Jackie nodded.

"Well. You were absolutely right about making a mistake in accepting training at L&B. We have four L&B refugees on staff already." She lifted one shoulder dismissively. "They're a big firm. If you play the game their way you'll be prominent in the field. They do a lot of work. We move in different circles."

Jackie nodded again. "Anyway, it seemed that if I wanted to take back some control over my career, I should look for a firm that ... suited my ideals more closely."

"Why us?" Angela was dispassionate again, regarding Jackie with a black marble gaze.

"The name of the firm intrigued me. When I called last night, I was going to get some information —"

"To look us over —"

"Basically. I don't want to leap before I look again."

"Let me see your resumé." Angela held out an imperious hand.

Jackie handed it over and then occupied herself by studying the project photographs on Angela's walls while she read. Her Taliesin-trained eyes liked what they saw — smaller, residential buildings. A lot of in-fill housing. Renovations of small apartment buildings and residential inns. NDA's projects appeared to range all over the greater Bay Area in a variety of neighborhoods. Jackie made a mental note of the locations of several of them so she could look up the specs.

"How's Dr. Joe keeping up with life?"

Jackie started, then smiled. "He's doing great." Her smile broadened as she recalled Taliesin West's oldest resident instructor and greatest story-teller. "He's simply amazing."

There was a glimmer of an answering smile from Angela. "It's been about fifteen years since I've seen him. I was doing research on-site." Angela returned her attention to the resumé. After a moment she extended her hand again. "Your portfolio."

Jackie crossed her fingers as Angela leafed through the pages. The Boston firm had let her take copies of the work she'd contributed to, and in her humble opinion, there were some fine conceptual designs included. Her graduate projects had been considered quite good. The last page was a handwritten note from Dr. Joe himself, telling her one of her graduate designs had received an honorable mention from a Japanese design school awards program. Somehow L&B had made her feel ashamed of having gone to "impractical" Taliesin when in fact it was something she was very proud of.

Angela grunted as she read the note and then closed the portfolio. For the next twenty minutes she rapid-fired questions at Jackie about several of the projects, testing her recall and understanding of high conservation and earthquake designs. Jackie felt her poise return as she answered. She was on solid ground in those areas. She might not have the imagination to design a butterfly bridge or Falling Water, but her ideas about the basics of building design had a creative flair and a solid grasp of practical engineering. She had never made the mistake of designing something without load-bearing walls, something Kelly had done twice.

When she finished her questioning, Angela drummed her fingers briefly on her desk. She studied Jackie for a moment, then said, "I know L&B doesn't pay associates in training much more than bus fare. We'd pay you a little better than that, but if you survive here, pass your exams and are asked to stay on as a full associate, your pay won't go up very much. The kind of work we do is not that lucrative and no one here, including me, lives in anything like a usual architect's style."

Jackie's heart was pounding. "Having seen the usual architect's style up close and personal, I can safely say it's a style I have no intention of adopting. And after living in a tent for three summers at Taliesin West, I've gotten used to the idea of living simply."

Angela smiled. "Can you spend another half-hour here?"

Jackie nodded. So she'd be late to work. She didn't care.

"Wait here a moment."

Angela walked briskly out to the main office, returning in a few minutes to lead Jackie to another office. "Diane, this is Jackie Frakes. Jackie — Diane Donahue. She's the preceptor with a vacancy. I'll leave you to talk."

Jackie shook hands with the red-haired Diane and they shared pleasantries. Diane reviewed her portfolio and her resumé but didn't probe as hard as Angela had. The gaze from deep hazel eyes, however, was as penetrating as Angela's had been. She commented wryly that Jackie had probably been grilled enough for one day. "You passed Angela's inquisition, so I won't do it to you again. When can you start?"

Jackie gulped. "You mean . . . um, well, how soon would you like me to?"

"Yesterday, but I know you'll have to give L&B notice." Diane made the same dismissive gesture with her shoulders that Angela had. She had probably picked it up from Angela. Plainly, Diane wouldn't give two cents about giving L&B notice.

"Can I have a day to decide? Is that okay?" All her instincts told her to say yes right away, but nonetheless, she knew that she should look into NDA's background. "If I decide to accept it'll be at the most two weeks until I could start."

Diane grinned. "That would be fabulous, but if you have to stay on another week, I'll understand. And I do hope you accept."

"I'll let you know first thing tomorrow morning," Jackie said. "Oh. I suppose we should talk about money before I make up my mind."

"What a novel concept," Diane said wryly. "I'm sorry. I should have brought it up — I thought Angela would have covered it."

"She said it would most likely be more than what L&B's giving me, but she wasn't more specific."

Diane named a figure that left Jackie with a pleased smile. Diane arched an eyebrow and said, "Get used to it. If you hang around this place it won't be going up any time soon. Angela's very fair about handing out bonuses when we have a good year, but the last couple have been tough. We're all in it together, though."

"That's encouraging," Jackie said. "I'm almost

certain I'll say yes, but I'll let you know as soon as I've had a chance to think about it — no later than tomorrow morning."

They shook hands again and Jackie left, feeling as though she was walking on air. Filled with surging confidence and hope, she decided she could risk being even later for work so she could check NDA's status with the American Institute of Architects.

She left the AIA offices on a cloud. Angela Martine and Diane Donahue were both members in good standing, NDA itself was a paid up member and voluntarily participated in peer assessment and review. They were in good standing with the California Board of Architects. She had no qualms about accepting the job and stopped at the pay phone in the AIA building lobby to call Diane Donahue and accept. She floated down to the MUNI train and then up the three blocks to the L&B building.

Mannings was very unpleasant when Jackie told him she was leaving, but admitted that Randall had been dubious about her future at L&B. He was downright nasty when she said she was going to NDA and reminded her specifically and at length about the ethics of taking any work she'd done for L&B to another firm. She assured him that she knew the ethical code as well as anyone at L&B and that she had not and would not discuss the drawings she'd done on the affordable housing project with anyone at NDA. In the end, they agreed she only needed to stay long enough to wrap up her CAD specifications for the condominium project. The following Friday was set as her last day.

Mary Nguyen was both congratulatory and dismayed. "I'm so happy for you, but Jesus, I'm going to miss having you around. This makes me the only female associate in training."

"I'm sorry, Mary, really."

Mary cocked her head to one side. "No, you're not. Why pretend? I wish you just the best of everything, you weasel."

Jackie laughed and promised to go out to dinner with Mary on her last day. Even when the memory of Leah intruded on her, she found herself savoring it instead of dreading it.

She was starting over. If this was as bad as it got, she could handle it.

She felt good until she remembered she would see Parker this weekend. She was not looking forward to it.

7

Leah muscled Butch to one side and answered the door. She knew that someone had been coming down the driveway because of Butch's barking. For a moment she let herself imagine it might be Jackie, but she quelled the thought. Jackie wasn't coming back, and Leah wasn't sure she wanted her to. It had just been one of those things — close quarters.

"So, the great Lee Beck answers her own door," a musical, mocking voice said.

"Constance!" Leah blinked stupidly and then stood back to let her in.

"And this is the old homestead. Quaint and cozy."
Constance pulled off her gloves and stomped her
boots on the mat where Leah's thick, practical winter
boots were piled. Long curls of blond hair fell around
her shoulders as she pulled her ski cap off. "No
wonder you never invited me up here. You'd never
get me away. Though your place in Hayward isn't
exactly chopped liver."

Leah closed the door and gave Constance a wry
glance. "So what are you doing here?"

"Not even glad to see me?" Constance cupped
Leah's face in her hand and gave her one of her
lingering kisses — the kind that had always peeved
Sharla even though Leah had never shown the
slightest interest in Constance's considerable charms.
For the first time Leah allowed to herself that now
she had the choice of whether to respond. She wasn't
sure what to do. So she backed away.

Constance laughed. "Same old Lee. I was in the
neighborhood, darling, and thought I'd find out what
my favorite artist is doing with herself."

Leah led the way into the kitchen. "You don't
expect me to believe that, do you?"

"But it's true, sweets. I'm staying at Kirkwood for
a few days and the skiing's bad today because of the
wind. So I thought I'd drive over and see you. Find
out if you're still alive. I got lost twice."

"You mean find out if I've got any more
commissions for you." Constance looked stricken for a
moment and Leah instantly regretted her flip tone.

Instead of her usual banter, Constance patted
Leah's cheek. "I've been worried about you."

The warmth of Constance's hand penetrated to
Leah's stomach. She was suddenly aware that it

wouldn't take much for Constance to seduce her. She'd been more than ready to go to bed with Jackie, who was straight, for God's sake, and here was Constance who had never made any secret of her desire for Leah.

"I know," she said at last. She stepped away from Constance's hand and heard her sigh. "Would you like some coffee?"

"If you're still hooked on gourmet blends, I'd love some." Constance's upbeat tone had returned. "So. Have you been working?"

"I only started to recently. You may be psychic, because I was going to send you some snapshots in a few weeks."

"Lee — you're kidding. I'm so happy for you. I know it's been tough, darling. Can I peek?"

Smiling indulgently, Leah led the way to her studio. She felt so good about the work she had no qualms showing it to Constance. Constance had a good eye for art and, importantly, an eye for what would catch critical opinion and what would sell — sometimes two completely different things. Leah wanted both.

As she opened the door she said, "The entire series is called *Painted Moon*. I had a houseguest over Thanksgiving —"

"A houseguest? Someone besides me?" Constance swept into the studio after Leah, taking her hand. Her tall, slender frame was rigid with indignation. She caught Leah's gaze and held it. "Who was it?"

"A woman who got lost in that big storm over Thanksgiving." She waved a hand as though the contact had meant nothing, hiding the fact that remembering Jackie still moved her pulse to an aerobic level. Her fingers still felt the sensation of Jackie's wetness surrounding them, her ears could still hear the moaned, fervent *Yes.* "Anyway, the moon came out in an eerie blue, almost as if it were painted by the snow. It really got my creative juices flowing."

"Is that all that got flowing?" Constance turned away, obviously not expecting an answer to her jibe.

"Your mind is always on one thing," Leah observed.

"Not that it ever did me any good with you. The only artist I've ever met who wasn't ready to hop into bed —" Her voice trailed away as Leah uncovered the first canvas. "Lee. My God."

"There are eight in the series. This is *Moon Pines.*"

Constance sank down to her knees to examine the bottom of the painting where streaks of silver meshed with thick whorls of pewter paint. "It's exquisite. Oh, darling, it's beautiful." Her tone was breathless and she seemed mesmerized.

Leah swelled with pleasure and felt tears start in her eyes. She trusted Constance's judgment and it touched her that Constance had lost her hard-boiled composure.

"The silver work — you should have been a metallurgist."

"It's aluminum with silver. I still have more to solder into place and then finishing, of course."

"There's something about the color. Women will go ape for these colors. You've always stuck with primaries before... The snow... How did you..." Constance began shaking her head. "Show me more."

Leah gave Constance all the time she wanted with

each canvas. Each one was as tall as Leah, and Constance studied every inch.

"If ever I wanted to keep something for the gallery, it would be this. You've obviously been working some long hours. But we're going to make a tidy fortune with these, darling."

Leah sighed. "I always feel sad about selling them. But that's life."

Constance turned from *After the Moon.* "I'm going to feel sad too. But as you say . . ." Her gaze fell on the covered easel. "What are you working on now?"

Leah tried to be nonchalant. "Just an experiment. I'm not ready to show it." She didn't want Constance to see the painting. She wasn't sure she wanted anyone to see it — especially Jackie.

For a moment, it seemed as though Constance would protest, but then she smiled indulgently. "If the surprise is as good as the ones I've seen, I can wait." She put her hands on her hips and regarded Leah with an open, appreciative smile. "You're better than ever, sweets."

Leah found herself responding to Constance's openness. "Thanks. So are you."

Constance made a noise of disbelief. "Is that a compliment? Is the reticent, hard-to-pin-down Lee Beck complimenting little ol' me?"

"I won't do it again if it bothers you so much," Leah said with a laugh.

"That's okay. I can handle it. So, are you inviting me to dinner?"

"If you stay that late, you may as well stay the night," Leah said slowly. She swallowed as Constance radiated happiness at the idea. She'd never seen the sophisticated, elegant Constance so open about what she felt. But then, she hadn't seen Constance for almost two years.

"Darling, you couldn't drive me away."

They settled in front of the Franklin stove after a simple dinner of bread and spaghetti. Constance was full of all the latest gossip — who had received grants and who hadn't. Who was sleeping around and who wasn't. Who had been the rage of the fall gallery shows and who hadn't. Constance knew everyone and everything about the art world. The Reardon Gallery was San Francisco's leading art house, and she had a dozen important art world discoveries to her credit, one of whom was Lee Beck.

Leah nonchalantly brought up the subject of Jellica Frakes. Not that she thought Constance even knew that Jellica had a daughter.

"She's getting the Fulvia Award this year. The ceremony's next weekend, I think. For her *Weavers* series."

The series that Jackie had mentioned. "Where's that on display?"

"It's on tour. London right now, I think. It'll be at MOMA in the city sometime next March, I think. Since when are you a Jellica fan?"

"Her daughter was my unexpected houseguest," Leah admitted.

"If she's anything like her mother . . . my, my. I met Jellica once and nearly died. She's gorgeous — in an Eleanor Roosevelt sort of way. I always wondered why her students mentioned her with such — not awe. Respect and high regard. And fondness. She was definitely handsome." Constance grimaced. "Happily married to a Canadian ambassador from a monied Quebec family. Too bad. Whenever anyone tells me they don't like her work I always probe at why and sure enough, it's envy."

"Jackie's not in the least like Eleanor Roosevelt," Leah said with a smile. "She's too . . . it's hard to describe. Her features are all ordinary, but she has expressive eyes. A deep green, almost dark gray. The way they fit is not pretty, but pleasing. Maybe her mouth is too wide. I sketched her and tried to figure it out."

Constance regarded her warily. "You're trying too hard to make it seem like it didn't matter, but she really shook you, didn't she?"

Leah nodded. "I should have known I couldn't lie to you. Yeah, she shook me. But like mother, like daughter. She's straight and in a relationship." Her nose should grow for that lie, she thought. No one who said *Yes* the way Jackie had could be satisfied with her relationship.

"Well, that's good," Constance said, her pale green eyes looking into Leah's. "Maybe there's room for me in your life now."

Leah blushed. "I'm starting to feel like a deer and you're the hunter."

"You're hardly defenseless, sweets. And I can't be coy with you. I want you too much." Constance's voice caught as though she was startled by the frankness of her admission.

Leah didn't know quite what to say. "You know, I've never really considered being with you."

Constance laughed with a hint of bitterness. "Sharla was always there. God, how you loved that woman. It made me crazy. There was never any room for anyone else. I always felt as though you wouldn't even let yourself like me."

The mention of Sharla didn't bring its usual stabbing pain. Leah sighed. Since Jackie had come and gone in her life, it hadn't. "I won't apologize for loving Sharla."

Constance turned sharply toward Leah. "Don't. I'd think less of you if you did. Just get on with your life. I'm offering..." She held out her hand and Leah slowly took it. "At least let me be your friend."

"You want more than that."

"Yes, but friendship is a start. It's more than I've had."

Leah considered the fair, delicate hand she held. Constance's fingers were long and slender, her nails trimmed and polished, her palm smooth and soft. "I can't offer you anything more," she said slowly. I'm a fool to keep thinking of Jackie, she thought. A fool to keep wanting her.

Constance's voice was tremulous. "Can you at least offer me your bed for the night?" Leah was amazed, awed even, by Constance's emotion. "No strings. I understand." She tightened her grip on Leah's hand.

In answer, Leah slowly kissed Constance's palm. She felt Constance shiver in response and her own body prickled with sensual awareness. "Let's go upstairs," she said quietly.

Constance broke the tense mood at the foot of the ladder. "I thought you said stairs."

Leah laughed. "Sorry. Think you can make it?"

Constance gave her a gamin grin. "If the climb will be worth the effort."

"Tell me tomorrow," Leah said, starting her climb with a laugh. She was glad that the mood had become a little less intense. As she pulled back the covers and switched on the electric blanket, she felt a wave of misgivings. Doing this wasn't fair to Constance.

Then Constance was sinking onto the bed and pulling Leah after her. "Kiss me."

It wasn't hard to obey the husky command.

Constance met her kiss eagerly, capturing and holding Leah's face. "You taste like I thought you would," she said. "Very nice."

Leah straddled Constance's waist and gave herself up to being explored. Constance's hands swept up Leah's ribs, then slid around her back, pulling Leah's black turtleneck out of her jeans. Leah felt a jolt of passion when Constance's fingertips brushed her bare back and she moaned, lowering her mouth to Constance's again.

A deep sigh rippled through Constance's body. Leah knelt over her, her skin chilling as Constance pulled Leah's turtleneck and undershirt over her head, then brought her warm hands back to Leah's shoulders. She stared up at Leah from the bed, her face framed by the pale gold of her hair. She bit her lower lip as her hands slid down and gently cupped Leah's breasts.

Every nerve in Leah's body goosepimpled. Her breasts felt swollen and she thrust them forward into Constance's hands.

Constance licked her lips and drew her breath in deeply. Her hands moved to the buttons of Leah's jeans, fumbling slightly with each until they were all undone. Her hands slid under the waistband and pushed the clothing down. She sat up, pushing Leah back until she could sit up. Then slid her hand unerringly to the center of Leah's passion.

Leah shuddered, and pulled Constance's mouth to her breasts. She'd been ready for this since Jackie ... unfair, unfair, she reminded herself. This is Constance, the first woman to touch you since Sharla. The only woman to touch you besides Sharla.

Constance. Leah gave herself up completely. She urged Constance inside her with slow undulations of her hips. She held Constance's mouth hard against her breasts, encouraging tender bites.

Constance held her tightly, her fingers stroking Leah's urgent need. "Come on," she whispered fiercely into Leah's breasts. "Come on."

Leah went rigid — too much sensation, too much pleasure. Another stroke inside her, then another and her body jerked, giving way to Constance's demand. Piercing yellow danced behind her clenched eyelids, mixed with waves of crimson and hyacinth. She cried out as she sank into Constance's waiting arms, then sobbed, "Oh God," into Constance's shoulder.

"Okay, it's okay," Constance whispered in her ear. "I'm sorry I went in so fast like that."

"No, no, don't be," Leah gasped. She shuddered again and managed to get a hold of her emotions. "I'd forgotten it could feel so good."

"It's been a long time for you," Constance said soothingly. "Let's get comfortable and take it slow."

Leah shook her head. "I don't want to go slow."

She rolled onto her side and unzipped Constance's slacks. Constance had beautiful legs — firm and lightly tanned. A birthmark graced the inner curve of one thigh, spoiling the perfection and making them that much more alluring.

Constance opened her legs and Leah settled between them. She nipped gently at the smooth lines where hip met thigh.

"Don't tease me," Constance suddenly whimpered. "Lee, I've waited too long."

The taste of Constance was like amber, like topaz. Musky, not sweet, heady, somehow dark. Leah swept her tongue inside, seeking deeply for Constance's essence and felt hands pressing her in. She fought the pressure and finally came up for air, then dove again into the depths of Constance's passion. Her pleasure at loving Constance intensified to rich sable. The brush of Constance's hair was soft as mink against her forehead.

When Constance finally pushed her away, Leah could only think how unlike Sharla, who had tasted of carmine, fuchsia and claret. Unbidden, still steeped in the scent of Constance, she wondered what Jackie tasted of. Then she mentally kicked herself for longing after a woman she'd never see again.

Constance came to her, her mouth hungry, and Leah gave up all thoughts of Sharla and Jackie. Tomorrow she might think of them again, but tonight belonged to Constance. She would feel guilty for using her tomorrow. But that was tomorrow.

She opened herself to Constance's loving attention.

Leah awoke to hear Constance muttering loudly about the "damned inconvenience" as she made her way down the ladder.

Her voice gravelly, she called out, "You get used to it."

"It's a good thing I don't have to pee urgently. I'd never make it, between the ladder and the fact that it's freezing in here." Feet thudded on the floor and Butch barked.

Leah sat up. It was after noon, and she hadn't fed Butch when she'd gotten up earlier in the morning. The house *was* cold, but this morning all that had been on her mind was a quick trip to the bathroom, brushing her teeth and then scrambling back into bed with Constance.

A dam had broken within her, and she knew that the bitter despair of losing Sharla was receding. She could still close her eyes and long for Sharla, hear her voice, imagine she smelled her. But the memories of their love were growing into a comforting blanket she could pull close when she needed the warmth. She still carried the regret and guilt of Sharla's drowning — maybe she'd never be rid of that. But Jackie had started her on the road to her future, and Constance had pushed Leah from a crawl to overdrive.

Butch made her feelings very plain as Leah scooped out food and set it down. The wounded, accusing glare from the expressive brown eyes moved Leah to defrost some of Jackie's turkey broth and spoon it over the kibble. Butch wolfed it down and then retired to the front of the kitchen stove, her nose in the air. Leah stoked up the stove and was finally rewarded with the thump of a tail on the floor.

She saw to the stove in the living room and then slipped into the bathroom as soon as Constance emerged from it, all pink from a shower and wrapped in Leah's robe.

She hurried through her shower and pulled on clean sweats. She caught her reflection for a moment in the fogged mirror. She wiped away the mist and stared at herself intently. Her lips had more color, her eyes were warm, the brown almost a dancing bronze.

She no longer looked like death. *Sharla, oh my love.* She blinked back the beginning of tears and saw her lips curve in a gentle smile.

Constance was huddled on the couch. "When does it get warm?"

"Very soon," Leah said. "I'm starving. I think it's time for lunch."

"Me too." Constance said. "All that activity," she added with a smirk.

Leah grinned. "You know, I'll bet the winds are still pretty high over at Kirkwood."

Constance lowered her gaze demurely. "You're probably right. It would be a waste to drive over there to see."

"Perhaps you should stay over another night."

"Perhaps I should," Constance said. The robe slipped open to frame Constance's alluring decolletage. She looked up at Leah through her light brown lashes. "I suppose you wouldn't take advantage of a poor maiden, now would you?"

Leah laughed wickedly. "I was planning to."

"Well, good," Constance said. She reclined on the couch, letting the robe fall open. "But you've got to warm it up in here. Or cover me with something. Preferably yourself."

It was no hardship to pull a half-naked Constance into her arms. For a while they pretended Leah was only trying to keep Constance's breasts out of the cold, and then that Leah was only trying to warm her hands between Constance's thighs. Then they were beyond pretense.

8

A sunny, winter day in the Bay Area meant sixty degrees and the temptation to put the top down on the MG. The fresh air would clear her head and Jackie needed her wits if she was going to talk to Parker honestly about their relationship. Her thick head was the result of having had a bit too much wine, dinner and dessert with Mary the night before.

After agreeing that she only had to work through the following Friday, Mannings had proceeded to load her with so much work she'd had to cancel last weekend with Parker. She hadn't made much of a fuss — she knew she also needed the time to work out what her feelings toward Leah meant. He had accepted her call with distracted resignation. His easy acceptance left her even more unsettled. After she hung up she realized he hadn't asked her why she was so busy.

Each time she had sent another CAD layout to the massive rendering printer she spent the minutes waiting for her screen to rebuild and thinking long and hard about Leah. And sex. And Parker. And commitment.

She had concluded that being cooped up in a cabin with someone could make anyone think they were attracted to that person. And everyone had sexual impulses. Yes, she was almost certain that the moments with Leah had been a fluke.

She would have felt better except for the "almost."

However she might have felt toward Leah or might feel toward women in the future had nothing to do with her feelings for Parker. With far more certainty she felt that he did indeed take her for granted. And she was sure her feelings did not have the strength to last a lifetime. Her parents' example had taught her to expect nothing less. She didn't know where that left her, but she did know that something between her and Parker needed to change. Either they would get stronger and tighter, which seemed unlikely, or break apart completely — and that idea scared her.

She put her energy into appreciating the beauty of the day. The Junipero Serra freeway was one of the loveliest in the entire area — it made the drives to San Jose bearable. The muted gold of the grass-covered hills and gray-green leaves of the eucalyptus trees glimmered in the brilliant golden sunshine. The sky was achingly blue. Abruptly she wondered what Leah would make of the light and color.

She tried getting angry with herself for reopening a topic she had decided to put aside, but her heart wasn't in it. So she made herself think about Parker.

What would she say to him? All her resolution faded away and she mentally kicked herself. Did she or didn't she want to end it with him?

What *did* she want, anyway?

Leah flickered into her thoughts. *It's like this between women . . .*

She stopped at the grocery store and bought some soda and muffins. She stood for a long time in front of the condoms, then reluctantly added a packet to her basket. She recognized that she was steeling herself for the prospect of having sex with Parker. Maybe everything would be all right if she did. Everything would go back to normal.

In front of the juice boxes she realized what she had told herself. That she felt abnormal. She had twisted her impulses until unwillingly having sex with Parker seemed normal while going blissfully and easily to Leah's bed was wrong.

She paid for the groceries and sat numbly in her car. If not for Leah, then how long might she have gone not recognizing her sexual desires? After she got married? Should she be glad it hadn't come to that? To have to leave someone because they were fundamentally the wrong partner? After she had children? Children . . . yes, she wanted to be a mother. As good a mother as her own had been. The world needed good parents.

Pieces of her life slipped into place. Finally, a whole emerged that made sense. If she wanted children, then she must want sex with men — that had been the false theory that had made her ignore what might have been with Kelly and look to Parker for her future.

A half-hour slipped away, then nearly another as she coped with the secret she'd uncovered. She pulled at the idea from all sides and it stayed intact. She was suspicious of it — it was too easy an answer. But it fit. It explained the choices she'd made the way nothing else did. She hadn't moved across the country for love, but to keep the choice of having a family open.

Stupid. She felt so stupid. She remembered now a billboard she'd seen in San Francisco featuring two women, one with her hand on the other's swelling tummy. The caption had said something about family values. She had thought it very San Francisco and cool. Inside she had felt confused and sad. Now she knew why. They'd figured out something she hadn't. Lesbians were around her everywhere, women with babies, sperm banks, ads for gay parent support groups — she'd seen it all and been absolutely oblivious about what it could mean for her.

Well now she'd seen what it could mean. She'd certainly taken her time, too.

* * *

She left the groceries in the car and went to Parker's apartment, unlocking the door with the key she'd already removed from her ring. He wasn't home yet. It was the matter of a few minutes' work to pack up the belongings that had accumulated in his place into a couple of grocery sacks. When they had moved out from Boston and needed to furnish two places they'd done most of the arguing about what belonged to whom. She could look back now and see that it had been the beginning of the end.

She carried the bags down to her car, then went back to the apartment to wait. She tried to think of what she would say, but nothing brilliant occurred to her.

His key in the lock startled her heart into her throat. The brief moment in which he smiled at her across the room gave her a shock. She had not known how she would feel when she saw him. She wondered if she had ever deeply loved him. No, she was beyond wondering. She knew that she had not.

But she hadn't expected to feel this way. As he crossed the room she remembered that he had an engaging laugh, and she saw once again that he was lean and attractive in a bookish, sleepy way. She was beset with memories of good, fun times. The museums they had prowled through together, the picnics and hikes, the moments of passion when she had been satisfied in his arms.

She deliberately made herself think of Leah. *It's like this between women . . .* The shudder in her stomach put her feelings for Parker into perspective. She didn't want to hurt him but it was over.

"Howdy, stranger." He dropped a friendly kiss on her cheek, then set his satchel and keys on the couch. He brushed his blond-brown hair out of his eyes. She opened her mouth to chide him about getting it cut, then stopped herself. She noticed he looked tired and pale — normally she would also chide him about not getting enough sleep or the right food. "How's it going?"

A deceptively simple question. Say something, she told herself, you're in your head too much. "Very strangely," she finally managed. She wouldn't do him any favors if she tried to lead up to things gently. "There are lots of things going on for me right now."

He nodded distractedly and then — deliberately, she realized — didn't look her in the eye.

For the first time she considered that maybe she wasn't the only one not entirely happy with the way their relationship was going. For a moment she felt something between jealousy and betrayal.

"I have a new job."

He did glance at her then. "Yeah? How'd that happen?" He sank onto the couch, but he didn't look comfortable.

Jackie sat down in the armchair and succinctly explained. He congratulated her and appeared to be listening, but his gaze was everywhere but on her while she talked. When her story trailed to an end he rambled about his software project, but his thoughts were disjointed, as though he couldn't concentrate. He sounded like she had while describing her new job. As though he didn't want to tell her too much because he didn't want her to be too interested. It suddenly seemed to her that neither of them was investing energy into something they both knew was dead.

They sat in silence for a few moments and Jackie fought against the overwhelming feeling of sadness in the pit of her stomach. Then Parker suddenly sat up and began talking to her instead of around her.

"I've been thinking." He slowly slid onto one elbow and leaned heavily on the arm of the couch. "Have you given any thought to where we're going? Us, I mean."

Perhaps a year ago she might have thought Parker was beginning a proposal of marriage. "Yes I have." She stared at his fingers, recalling his touch on her. Should she feel revolted? She didn't — she just recognized that he didn't move her to the heights she now suspected existed. "We don't seem to have any . . . sizzle left," she said finally.

Parker heaved a sigh of relief. Jackie thought it needn't have been quite so heartfelt. "I know what you mean," he said.

She straightened her spine and took a deep breath. "Let's not drag it out, okay? The regrets I have were all my own doing."

He stared down at the coffee table and Jackie saw his lower lashes dampen. "I'm sorry," he said.

She reached across the gap between them and covered his hands with her own. "Don't be. I think we can say it's mutual. I . . . I came to a decision before I got here today. I've already gathered my things. I'm sorry too."

"Is there someone else?"

It's like this between women ... Her heart thumped hollowly as she answered. "No one particular person. But I've —"

"There is for me. I feel real bad about it. I ... we went out for the first time last weekend and something happened and I couldn't lie to you. You're too fine for that. I just can't ... I can't be with you again. I want to be with her." His regret came through strongly. She sensed he was telling her the truth. She knew that he needn't have told her anything and was glad of his honesty. It called for honesty from her in return.

"It's okay. I think ..." Jackie swallowed then continued. "I think we both knew it was ending and it opened our eyes to new possibilities. I hope she is everything you need."

"I hope you find happiness too." He squeezed her hands.

Jackie realized that she could avoid telling him she was attracted to women. She could slide out of his life and he could never know. But what if he found out later? Would he think something stupid, like that he had made her turn gay? And in the end maybe she didn't care what he knew and didn't know, but she cared how she felt about herself. He'd been honest with her. Besides, if she couldn't tell Parker she would have trouble telling other people.

Not telling anyone didn't occur to her.

"I do have something I feel I should tell you." She released his hands and sat back in her chair. "I want you to know the whole truth. I think I ... I prefer women. I think I'm a lesbian."

He stared at her blankly for a long moment, then pulled his hands away. Then he blinked and shook his head. He paled, then flooded with color all along his forehead and cheekbones. "What?"

"I think I'm a lesbian." She said it without a quiver.

"You *think* you're a . . . you think you like women in bed? Have you . . . you know?"

She shook her head. "But near enough to realize I've been blind to some feelings I've always had."

"Was I that bad in bed?" He sounded lost and hurt.

"No. I knew you'd think that," she said, her tone growing more acerbic. "It's not about you. It's about what I feel. I enjoyed what we did in bed." It was a little white lie because she hadn't always wanted to have sex when he did. She promised herself that faking passion would go the way of the condoms.

"Then why? I just don't understand." There — that was the Parker she had known lately. His chin was out and he was sure she had wronged him. He had looked just that way when she had suggested that he might be able to afford their last trip to the movies. But, no, they always went fifty-fifty, he'd said. Their relationship was equal, he'd said.

"Why are you in love with someone else? Why does anyone prefer sex the way they do? There's a million ways to do it, and a million ways I haven't even thought of. All I know is that when I go looking for someone to be in my life I'll be looking for a woman." She patted his hands again but he slid them out from under hers. "I hope . . . I hope you can still wish me happiness."

His mouth twisted in an ugly grimace. "I can hope you come to your senses."

"Don't be a jerk," she said sharply. "I can hope you're happy."

"I will be. It's normal, after all."

Jackie opened her mouth to argue, then snapped it closed. She didn't know what to say. She was ill-prepared to argue the virtues of a lifestyle she hadn't even tried yet. She gave him The Look — it was the best she could do on short notice.

His Adam's apple bobbed. "Let's not fight about it."

Jackie sighed. "I'm not leaving you for another woman, you know. We're leaving each other. And you're the one with someone else."

He stared stonily at her for a moment then said, "So it's goodbye, then."

Her own goodbye lodged in her throat, making it ache.

She pulled off the freeway in Palo Alto, put the top down and took the long way home. The crimson and bronze sunset from the Pacifica cliffs promised a cloud-free tomorrow.

♥ ♥ ♥ ♥ ♥

The light in the cabin was bad. It was cold. The trips to town for supplies took too long. Washing brushes left the unpleasant odor of thinner hanging in the air, particularly in the loft. The stoves were tiring to maintain. She'd tried making biscuits and burned them to the point of having to throw out the pans.

She had even written a letter to her parents, not saying much beyond the depth of the snow and that she was getting by on her own. Her parents had made their disapproval of Sharla plain. Unlike Sharla's parents, however, they hadn't told her she was dead to them — they just couldn't see Leah unless she reformed. When she had written to say Sharla had died, her mother had responded with a beautifully copied text of a Brethren hymn accompanied by a gentle note of regret. She had even said that she understood Leah's grief. Since then, corresponding with her parents had been easier. They made no demands of each other. She was able, after all the years of frost, to wish them a joyous Christmas.

Her own Christmas was deadly dull and she missed the trappings of a big meal and someone to share it. On the days she was honest with herself, she admitted that it was Jackie she missed. For the first time since Sharla's death, Leah felt cramped in the cabin. Cramped and cranky. Even the clank of Butch's collar was getting on her nerves.

Wearily, she dropped a load of wood next to the kitchen stove. Her listless gaze fell on the phone. Completely on impulse, she looked up Maureen's phone number and dialed without giving herself the chance to think twice.

"The house is fine," Maureen told her soothingly. "The housekeeping service has been very conscientious. No intruders. I've left the garden alone like you said, but really, it needs some help before spring. Valentina knows a great gardener." Maureen's lulling tone was sensuous. It was completely unconscious on Maureen's part, and more than one woman had delighted in just listening to her, Leah included.

"I think I'll be coming back pretty soon," Leah said. "I'll do it . . . it'll be good therapy."

"You're probably right. It'll be good to see you. Val and I have been worried."

"I'm better. I still feel — like half a person. But . . . well, anyway. I'm coming back. Coming home again."

"I can't wait to see you, Leah. Call me the moment you get in. I can't wait." Maureen sighed breathily into the phone. She did it with such innocent sincerity that it made Leah smile. Two years away from her friends — what had kept her away from the people she and Sharla had loved?

The prospect of going back to her lonely afternoon made Leah search for another topic. "How did the AIDS Dance-a-thon do this year?"

"I didn't go, but I heard it was a fun party," Maureen began. She summarized the income and expense, and dropped names and news in the categories of Brought in Big Bucks, New People on the Scene, Important Lesbians, the Intimate Friends of Important Lesbians, and Prima Donnas. Maureen was a volunteer in nearly 100% of the hours she didn't spend at her middle-management job in a large insurance company. She had at her fingertips the names of hundreds of people raising money for AIDS, breast cancer, domestic violence, experimental theater and lesbian and gay arts projects. Leah had gotten to know Maureen after Maureen had convinced her to be a jurist for a lesbian art show. "So if you're coming home I'll expect you to be there, okay?"

"I'm sorry, where again?"

"You haven't been listening to me at all, have you? I'm talking about the AIDS Foundation dinner."

"Is that all?" Leah smiled to herself.

"Of course not. I'll hit you up for about one event a month. Get you into circulation again."

"I'm not sure I want to circulate," Leah said. Going to dinners and dances alone would be a trial. She was also uncertain about how Constance fit into her future life.

Maureen tsk-ed. "Of course you do. I'll make sure you meet people who are fun to talk to. More than talk you'll have to arrange for yourself." Maureen's tone took on a definitely suggestive edge.

Leah rolled her eyes at the kitchen stove. "I'm definitely not in circulation for that. Not yet."

"Can't be a nun forever."

"From what I hear, some nuns have plenty of sex. Now, who told me that?" Her voice was bland.

Maureen had a wicked laugh. "Well, I suppose I do know something about nuns and sex. Having experienced Valentina's rapture repeatedly over the last six years."

When Leah hung up nearly an hour later Maureen had pinned her down for several events and extracted a firm promise to come to dinner so that Valentina could practice her latest recipes.

She snapped her fingers and Butch left her spot near the stove to nuzzle at Leah's knees. "Want to go home, girl?"

Butch's ears pricked up and her wagging tail made emphatic yesses in the air.

"Yeah? Me too."

9

1-900-HOT-BUTT.

Jackie dropped the newspaper as though her fingers were burned. Her cheeks flamed and she picked it up again, carefully arranging the pages so she didn't see the explicit photograph of a male posterior and the phone number again.

She read a review of a Theater Rhino production, then decided she needed another café latte. She made her way across the crowded patio to the coffee bar and placed her order. So this was Sunday afternoon in Noe Valley.

Her studio was in a less fashionable part of the Glen Park district, but it was easy by transit to get to Noe Valley — the part of the city that overflowed with lesbians. She knew that from reading the weekly alternative press. The men went to the bars in the Castro and the women went to coffeehouses in Noe Valley. At least that's what the advertisements implied. Now that she was experiencing the Noe Valley coffeehouse scene firsthand Jackie wasn't sure what she had thought she'd find.

Armed with her latte, she reclaimed her chair and went back to reading the gay weekly paper she'd picked up at the door. The calendar section detailed many holiday events for gays and lesbians, including a Messiah sing-along with the lesbian and gay choruses of San Francisco, which sounded like fun. There was a women-only dance on Christmas Eve to stave off the holiday blues, and a businesswomen's group was having dinner and a White Elephant gift exchange on Christmas Day at a posh restaurant.

The gay and lesbian community seemed determined to provide everyone with something to do over the holidays. Since Jackie wasn't going to be able to spend them with her folks, she appreciated the variety. After a moment she realized that there were probably many people whose families wouldn't welcome them if they tried to go home. She felt a tremor — what if her parents reacted like so many?

She forced the apprehension away. No, she had always stood firm on the foundation of their love for her. It was concrete with rebar and earthquake-proof. Perhaps her certainty in their unswerving support was making this change in her life easy. Well, easier.

She spent too much time thinking about it to make it easy.

The news stories went into detail about items such as child custody cases, local legislation and updates on what fundamentalists were doing in other states to restrict gay civil rights. She found the last type of story the scariest news she'd read in a long time. Didn't these people have better things to do with their time than worry about whom their neighbor was sleeping with?

She turned the page again and was presented with a view of another rear end — good God, she was seeing more of this model than she'd ever seen of Parker. The headline on a personal ad caught her eye: *Hung Hunk Hankers for Head.*

She grimaced. It wasn't that she was a prude — well, maybe she was. It's just that she didn't think that a few breathless moments with every nerve in her body yearning for another woman's touch meant her entire life was about sex. What about... affection? Trust? The real L-word — Love?

Her mother had always said that when the critics are out to get you, you have to put on a brave front. Maybe that's what these ads were all about. They made an interesting contrast — on the right was freewheeling sex. On the left a photo of a fundamentalist throwing acid at gay rights demonstrators.

Her common sense spoke up. You know, Jackie, you have a new job and lots of stress and strain right now. There's no point in trying to figure this all out in a day. Why not go home and make a reservation for the Christmas dinner? And just concentrate on work for a while?

She frowned again. The reason she was sitting in this coffeehouse was because she didn't know how to spend weekends in her studio. It didn't feel like a home and she now realized that part of the emptiness she had felt with Parker had been the lack of a shared home. Her roots weren't in her apartment and she felt adrift.

To fill time, she'd spent all of yesterday composing a two-line note to include with Leah's gloves. That at least was done. Today the apartment had seemed cold and dark. It was too soon to feel lonely, but if she gave it half a chance, she would.

She wasn't ready for Noe Valley. At that idea she smiled. She certainly wasn't ready for the Castro. At 27, she was definitely a member of the "older crowd" in the coffeehouse and one of a few with monotone hair. Her black jeans were okay, but the Shetland sweater did not exactly fit in. She wondered if the local AIA chapter had a gay/lesbian bulletin board on Internet. She smiled again. Now that was a good idea.

"I didn't know you lived around here!"

Jackie glanced up in surprise and found Mary Nguyen giving her a lopsided smile. After exclaiming over the coincidence of running into Mary, she said, "I thought you lived in the Sunset."

"I do, but I had a date. Come join us," she said with sincerity. Mary nodded toward a slender, mid-twenties Filipino woman who nodded back at Jackie and sent a look that said Jackie shouldn't even consider joining them. Jackie smiled to herself. San Francisco had a lot more lesbians in it than she'd ever had cause to notice.

"I don't think so, but thanks. I've just finished

my second cup and should head for home." Jackie stood up.

"Can I ask a stupid question, then?"

"Okay." Jackie had a feeling she knew what was coming.

"Where's what's-his-name?"

Jackie chewed on her lower lip, then realized she didn't feel self-conscious about it. "There is no what's-his-name anymore. And I don't think there'll be any more what's-his-names."

Mary's eyebrows shot up. "Well! I . . . I did wonder, you know. When we first met. But then I wonder about most women." She laughed engagingly.

"I haven't exactly crossed the Rubicon yet, but I'm definitely on the bridge," Jackie said. "Ever since I broke up with Parker I feel okay. Happy."

Mary stared at her intently. She grinned suddenly. "Let's have dinner again, okay?"

Jackie found herself grinning back, feeling a little lightheaded. "Yes, I'd like that. Um, well. Let's try again with the work-masks off. Do you still have my number at NDA?"

"Definitely. Well, I'll call you. Tomorrow."

Jackie picked up her newspaper and said goodbye, then wandered to the bus stop. Uncertain tomorrows stretched ahead of her, but she could meet them with her eyes wide open and only an occasional blink.

♥ ♥ ♥ ♥ ♥

Butch nosed the door open as soon as Leah unlocked it. With a bark, she scampered around the ground floor of the house, sniffing the corners and reacquainting herself with the furniture. She leapt up the stairs to the second floor, then barreled back down them to whine at the back door, wanting to go out.

Leah laughed and let her out, then followed Butch into the backyard. She grimaced. Maureen had been right. The yard was overgrown and unkempt, which Sharla would have hated.

Still, a bright row of purple and white crocuses lined the walk and daffodil bulbs were beginning to break the soil behind them. Unthinkable in the mountains.

Butch was busily marking the two trees. She would probably wander down the fence and get in the stickers and then come back wanting to be brushed. Leah sighed with something like contentment. Sharla was gone, but some things — like the doggie love of getting dirty — didn't change.

She went back inside and was glad that it was clean and presentable. She didn't want to spend any time on housekeeping, not with ideas bottled up for the last two years aching to seep out through her fingertips. A new start on New Year's Day.

She hauled in her suitcases and boxes, then unloaded the canvases. One by one she carried them around the back to the studio, feeling immediately comfortable in its orderly confines. She noticed that she had several new neighbors — the neighborhood had become more prosperous-looking since she'd left it two years ago for the seclusion of the cabin. She wrinkled her nose. Suburbia had caught up with her.

Hayward was not a fashionable address, but it was one of the least costly Bay Area places to have a view and enough room for privacy. Her house perched on the edge of a deep canyon filled with pines and eucalyptus. In the summer the air was fresh and clean and fog was something she watched blow into Berkeley, far to the north. In the distance San Francisco sparkled in the bright sunlight, but it couldn't be called a city view — hence the reduced price. As she took note of the BMWs and Volvos that now dotted the driveways she realized that other people had figured it out, too.

The riding school was still in business. Its gates were painted fresh white as always and stood open at the dead end of the block. She paused for a moment and listened. Children were playing somewhere near-by. A horse was being exercised, its hooves making a steady clop-clop rhythm on packed earth. The wisteria rustled in the breeze. A bee buzzed lazily not far from her ear.

What was missing was the sound of Sharla busy in the kitchen or on the phone, pestering gallery owners about forwarding commission payments, booking exhibits, making reservations. She had been a tireless agent and had had good business sense. She had insisted on buying a house as an investment, then gone about having the perfect artist's studio built in the large backyard.

Leah knew why she had dreaded coming back here — this was home. Where she would miss Sharla the most. A place that screamed for two people to fill it. In all her life she had never lived alone until the two years at the cabin. But the cabin was small and it had been easy to fill up the space.

Butch barked at her from the door of the studio. Lucky for Leah, she seemed to recall she wasn't allowed inside. "You're not half as dirty as I thought you'd be," Leah told her. She barked again and disappeared back down the hillside. Well, Butch seemed happy to be home.

She was just unloading the last canvas when a peach and white '57 T-bird cruised to a smooth halt at the curb. Constance's pride and joy, after her art collection.

"You're a welcome sight," Leah called to her, and she meant it.

Constance was sparkling with good humor. She opened the tiny trunk and produced a picnic basket. "I knew you wouldn't have had time to stock up on any food, so I stopped for your favorite things."

"I brought a few things," Leah said. "Food for Butch, mostly. She gets really cantankerous when she's hungry."

"As if you don't!" With a laugh, Constance disappeared into the house. Leah took the last canvas around the back. She heard Constance in the kitchen and discovered her unloading burgers, fries and onion rings from the hamper, along with sodas.

Leah laughed. "You are a doll, did you know that? I haven't had fast food in ages!"

"Just trying to make myself indispensable." Constance helped herself to some fries.

They settled at the Shaker-style dining room table, Constance saying, "I have some fabulous news."

"Do tell." Leah unwrapped a burger and bit into it. Delicious. She could feel her arteries going into shock even as she swallowed the first bite.

"Well, good news for you, bad news for Henry Eli. He broke his arm skiing and won't be able to get his show finished for the March opening. So you can have the three weeks, if you want them. You're practically finished with the *Painted Moon* series, aren't you?"

Leah gulped. "Yeah . . . almost. It came together so quickly. I have more metal work to do, but that won't take long. I'm anxious to get on with the next project."

"When do I get to see it? You've been so secretive."

"Not yet. It's too different. I don't feel confident about it yet."

"Okay. I'm dying of curiosity, though."

Leah ate another onion ring. "Thanks for bringing this. Thanks . . . for being here."

"Any time." Constance put a hand on Leah's arm. "I'm here for you in any way you'd like."

Leah had a hard time swallowing.

"It wasn't so bad, was it, the time we spent at the cabin?"

"It was fabulous."

Constance sat back and stared at Leah gloomily. "Then why do you look like you're going to cry?"

"I don't feel —" Leah blinked rapidly. "I love you as a dear friend. But I don't think I'll ever come to love you the way you want me to. I'd be cheating you."

"What if I don't mind?"

"You would."

Constance glanced down, hiding a smile. "I always forget you're you. That religious upbringing. Dearest, I'm not offering you lifetime commitment. I can't give you what *she* gave you. I'm here to be your friend, to share your bed if you like. I would certainly like it." She gave a half-laugh, part chagrin, part amusement. "I am not a one-woman woman, but I am very choosey about affairs. I've been having an affair with one woman for over fifteen years. We see each other annually."

Leah didn't know what to think. Trying to make a joke of it, she said, "So I would be part of the harem?"

Constance laughed again, but with exasperation. "You're not getting the point. No ties, no rules, no exclusiveness. I don't mean to make it sound like there are hundreds of women. Just a few — like you — women who . . . turn me on. I don't know how else to say it."

Leah gazed at Constance, asked in a low voice, "Are you safe? I mean . . . we didn't . . . I should have asked about —"

"I had a scare about six years ago and since then I've been careful. I know I'm okay and I certainly knew you hadn't been active — and neither of us do drugs, let alone share needles — so I didn't use anything. You don't have to worry about it." She crossed her legs and stared at the table. "It won't work, will it? Like I said, I keep forgetting you're you. All I see are your hands — you have fabulous hands, darling — and well," she went on, sounding philosophical, "I have a very pleasant memory. I hope you do, too."

Leah managed a slight smile. "Yeah, I certainly do. I don't regret it."

"Well, that's something." Constance blinked rapidly for a moment. "I have to run — there's a gala tonight. Oh, would you like to go the Women's Foundation benefit with me? I already have the tickets and don't feel like asking anyone else. Next Friday. Don't tell me you're booked. Wear that purple jacket. Darling . . ." Constance reached over to pat her hand. "I still very much want to be your friend. I hope it's not spoiled."

"No, it's not spoiled," Leah said sincerely. "I'm not sorry it happened, if you're not. And yes, I'll be there Friday."

She waved at the T-bird as Constance pulled away. She was glad that she and Constance were back on their old footing. All this time she thought Constance was looking for a settled life — what an ego you have, she chided herself. She needed friends more than lovers and between Constance and Maureen she'd be busy. Busy enough to not miss Sharla as much as she might have. Besides, there was also her work to absorb her.

Back in the studio, she uncovered the one canvas she wouldn't show to Constance and set it on the easel. The blue and silver of Jackie saying yes.

♥ ♥ ♥ ♥ ♥

"I can't believe I fell on my feet. I like everyone I've worked with and they expect me to work with clients and show initiative. They ask my opinion and listen to me. And they don't say I'm dumb when I say something really obvious. And Diane, my boss, seems to enjoy explaining things. She loves questions. And the projects are interesting. It's all working out." Jackie realized she had been babbling, but her mother didn't look bothered by it.

She had arrived in Dallas late the previous night

121

to find a room waiting for her and a bouquet of wildflowers with a note saying, "Room service for breakfast tomorrow so we can talk! Ring me around 8:30. — XXOOXX Mom." It had been a splendid idea. Her mother's first demand had been to hear all about Jackie's new job.

Jellica Frakes looked up from buttering her English muffin. "I'm so glad they appreciate your worth. And that you're learning. That other place didn't seem to want to teach you anything but how to run their computer. Drink your milk," she added, making one of her lightning changes from mentor to mother. Jackie grinned and took a big swallow.

"How does Parker feel about the big change in your life?"

Jackie wiped away her milk moustache. "He didn't really say. It sort of got lost in the shuffle of our breaking up."

"Jackson!" Her mother put down the muffin. "Why didn't you call me? Oh dear, I put my foot in it, didn't I? When did this happen?"

"I was wondering how to bring it up, so I'm glad you asked. We broke up before Christmas. I had made up my mind and he was also trying to tell me he met someone else. It was mostly agreeable."

Her mother's hazel eyes darkened, as though the sun had gone behind clouds. "I'm so sorry. You gave up so much."

Jackie gave her mother a wry look. "Well, if you promise not to let it go to your head, I'll tell you that you were right about him, and moving and going to L&B to work."

Her mother's steady gaze was tinged with sadness. "I didn't want to be right, you know."

122

"I know. But really, I feel great. I haven't felt this good since graduate school."

"There's something you haven't told me, though. I sense a secret of some sort." She took a bite out of her muffin and studied Jackie.

Jackie's jaw dropped. "You are a mind reader. It's *not* fair."

"I can't read all minds, just yours. And your father's."

"I knew it. Yes, there's something else."

Jackie didn't know how to start and into the long pause, Jellica said, "You can tell me anything, you know."

"Well, remember Thanksgiving? I told you I spent the weekend mostly with Lee Beck?"

Her mother nodded and her face stilled almost as though she could sense what was coming.

"Something happened." Jackie closed her eyes for a moment. "Not much of something happened, but enough. Enough for me to figure out that I'd rather be with women." She looked into her mother's perfectly still face and held her breath.

"Are you sure, *cherie*?" Jackie could feel the intensity of her mother's stare. "Do you feel like you have a choice?"

Jackie bit her lower lip, then sighed. "Oh, I don't know. Of course I have a choice. Of course I can choose not to act on my urges. But I have no control over the urges themselves. The way I feel when I think about her. I didn't choose to want a woman like I do." She pressed her palms to her eyes for a moment, then looked back at her mother. "I didn't choose this. But I can choose how to respond to it."

"And — how will you?"

"I . . . I want to taste the forbidden fruit." She smiled ruefully, realizing she sounded Victorian. "I think I'll probably make it a steady diet."

Her mother sighed somewhat sadly. "And I take it you're pretty sure it won't give you hives?" A smile lurked at the edge of her mouth.

Jackie started to respond, caught her breath, found her cheeks growing warm at the mere memory.

Her mother said, "Don't tell me, it's written all over you. It was fabulous."

"I think it would be if I actually *did* anything." Jackie laughed wryly. "If not Leah, then somebody else — a woman. That's the point. That women will be in my life from now on. I told you I went out for Christmas dinner and I let you think it was with Parker, I'm sorry about that. I didn't mean to lie. I just wanted to see you face-to-face."

"I understand, don't worry about it."

"I did go out. To a dinner party for lesbians. We had a lot of fun and I made some friends."

"And what about Lee Beck?"

"I'll probably never see her again," Jackie said. "I was scared. And she's still grieving for her lover."

Her mother nodded. "Oh, that's right. I'd forgotten she'd lost her girlfriend, well — more than a friend, obviously. Lover, agent, business manager. She never made an issue of her sexuality. Most people forget, I think."

"So anyway, she said I wasn't ready."

"Were you?"

Jackie gave her mother a sheepish look. "Mom, I was *ready*. I'm still ready. I've never been so ready."

Her mother smiled fondly. The sun came out in her eyes again. "Darling, I won't lie and say this isn't a shock. It is. Your father will have to get used to the idea, but of course, there's no question — I love you, your father loves you. And I'm glad to see you alive and awake and aware of what you're choosing. Even if you never see her again, you've still woken up. I knew something was missing for you, dear." Jellica's voice broke. "I didn't know how to help you find it. And I so much wanted you to find it."

"Damn," Jackie said. "I'm going to cry." She blotted her eyes with the table napkin.

Her mother cleared her throat and said, "I remember when I fell in love for the first time, I felt just like you do. I didn't have a choice about how I felt. I loved who I loved. And it was the most torrid, shameless affair I'd ever had."

"What happened?" Jackie dabbed one last time and concentrated on her mother.

Her mother grinned and leaned forward confidentially. "Well, my friends told me he'd be the ruin of me, he'd squash every artistic impulse I ever had and lead me into a life of pure boredom. And his friends were telling him I'd be the ruin of him, get him labeled a radical, ruin his chances for promotion." She shook her head sadly. "In the end . . ."

"What? What happened?" Jackie heard the scoop on this part of her mother's life.

"Well. What could I do? Like you said, I might not have chosen to feel like I did, but whether I acted on those feelings was really up to me. So I married him."

Jackie flopped back in her chair. "You're talking about Daddy," she said, wrinkling up her nose. "No fair. Everyone knows you have the perfect marriage."

"It would be a mistake for you to assume it has always been perfect. Or that perfect is easy. It took work, believe me. My work is fortunately portable, so I could go with him wherever he went." She leaned forward to pat Jackie's hand. "But what a remarkable work of art we produced."

Jackie blushed and tears swam in her eyes again. "Thanks."

"I hope you find happiness, dear. It's always been my wish for you." She leaned back and waved one hand airily. "And Parker was not going to make you happy." Not for the first time Jackie wished for her mother's gift of conveying worlds of meaning with a casual gesture.

After that, her mother seemed content to munch on her breakfast and talk about life in Lisbon. Jackie finished her muffin and had some strawberries.

"Well," her mother said briskly, as soon as the last of the berries had been eaten. "What are you going to do with yourself while I spend the day being dragged from gallery to gallery and feted at every turn?"

"I don't know. I wish I could drive out into the country somewhere. Just to see what it feels like. The sky is so big. And I didn't expect so many trees."

"Rent a car for the weekend, my treat. I know you told me not to feel bad about Christmas but I do. Find us someplace fun to go to tomorrow since all the festivities will be over. I'd love to hear some live jazz, I miss it. When do you have to fly out?"

"Not till Monday evening. Angela said it was okay

for me to take Monday off even though I've only been there a few weeks. She's a veritable lion, but we get along okay."

"Maybe I can meet her when I come out there in February."

"You're coming to San Francisco?" Jackie sat up with pleasure.

"Didn't I say — oh no, of course. I hadn't even gotten around to telling you. The *Weavers* is debuting at the Museum of Modern Art and they want me to do a benefit gala thing. I said yes primarily because I could spend some time with you. I'll plan on staying at least a week."

"My studio's really tiny, but I make great coffee."

"Nonsense, dear, I'll stay in a hotel. You can stay with me if you want and pretend you're on holiday. I wasn't looking forward to seeing Parker, so that's just as well." Her mother stopped, then blurted out, "I'm so glad you're not with him anymore."

"I'm glad, too," Jackie said with a smile.

"Anyway," Jellica continued in her brisk tone, "if you are with — if there's someone you're dating, I shall want to meet her, you know. That will never change."

"I've been going out with someone, but we're just friends. She's showing me the ropes, so to speak." Her mother laughed. "Oh, I'm so pleased you're coming to visit. It'll be great."

"Now go away, dear, and let me put on my face. Enjoy your day and I'll see you around seven before the banquet, okay?"

"Okay. And you don't need a different face." She

gazed fondly at the hazel eyes and salt-and-pepper hair. "I can only hope to be as beautiful as you are when I'm fifty-three."

"Out," her mother ordered.

10

Jackie was able to rent a car through the concierge who also gave her maps. Clad in black leggings, Reeboks and a bulky, warm sweater, she felt ready to explore.

She picked up the car and was pleased to find it was a little sports coupe. The highways around Dallas looked straight and flat on the map. She hadn't driven really fast since the last time she'd been in Germany. The clerk at the rental agency said the Texas highway patrol tended not to be much interested in anything under seventy-five — unlike California, where paranoia set in at sixty. She could whisk some cobwebs out of her mind and really get out into the country. Which direction out of Dallas? West toward Lubbock? Country-western songs began to play in her head. North toward Oklahoma City?

A town called Norman caught her eye. Norman, Oklahoma. Now where had she heard of that before? She concentrated for a moment and Leah's voice came back to her. *Sharlotte Kinsey from Norman, Oklahoma. Can you imagine being from a place so off the beaten track that the main sight for miles is an oil field?*

Unwilling to name what motivated her, Jackie set off for Norman, Oklahoma, her camera and map handy. She would spend most of the day driving there and back, but she loved exploring by car. Wildflowers. How people built their homes in different terrains. It would be a nice break.

The land was flat and soaked with rain, with no crops to break the unending stretch of dark orange clay. Gray clouds stretched overhead into the dim, charcoal horizon, leaving Jackie feeling very small and wondering about the native peoples who had roamed under the vast sky. How easy it would be think this was the entire world.

She eased herself into a caravan of cars and trucks all doing about eighty miles per hour. Sedate, by German standards, but it was exhilarating. The music was mostly country, but she didn't mind. She sang when she knew the words and drank in the red and gray countryside. She would build houses low to the ground with soft, rounded lines to merge into the hard horizon.

It was about three hours later when she stopped at a diner on the main drag into Norman. The town was not as small as she had thought it would be, but perhaps it had grown up since Sharla had lived here. She found herself asking the waitress about cemeteries. There were two, she discovered, and so she set off again.

The first cemetery looked disused and overgrown with no signs of any recent activity. She walked around a little and found deaths recorded only as recently as the 1930s. An icy wind cut quickly into her sweater and she gladly went back to the car.

The second cemetery was obviously in use. The size of it intimidated her. There was a funeral under way off to the right, so she parked some distance away and walked in that general direction in the hope that it was a more recently used part of the grounds. Some landscaping had created small rises and there were middle-aged oak trees here and there, which cut down the wind.

She wandered for a while, finding graves from the 1980s, but none more recent. The funeral was ending and people were leaving. She waited until only the funeral home attendants were left and then asked for their help.

The men, in their stiff black suits, looked her up and down. Jackie guessed she looked a little odd for a cemetery. Well, she probably looked a little odd for Oklahoma. She bent the truth and said she was looking for a friend from church camp. The men directed her to a general area where her school friend might be buried.

The graves along the path they'd directed her to were of the right time period. *Beloved daughter.*

Beloved wife. Beloved father. James, gone too soon. Carolyn, our loving sister.

Abruptly she realized she was looking at the right name.

Sharlotte Jean Kinsey. A simple, large cross in relief. At the bottom: *God be merciful to me a sinner.*

She looked at it for a few minutes, her fists clenching and unclenching. She was hot all over with rage — a deep burning anger the likes of which she'd never felt before.

To sleep here forever with such words over her — Jackie was at a loss. It was a shock to see the condemnation etched in stone. For her whole life she had been nothing but loved by her parents. She didn't have any enemies. Another shock hit her — these people would think the same of her, and they didn't even know her. She swallowed around the knot in her throat. No one had ever hated her before.

She thought about what her mother had said about making choices. So. She was choosing love and choosing to be hated, too.

She walked back to the cemetery entrance and around the corner to the florist that made its trade from mourners. She couldn't take a picture of the marker without something that showed that Sharla had been loved, deeply and truly loved.

Roses? No. Carnations? No. Gladioli — that was better. Scarlet glads, and some royal purple irises. Much, much better, she thought. She bought an armful of the most vivid blooms and a tall vase, refused the complimentary cross to hang from the bouquet, then carried them back to the cemetery.

The brilliant colors hid most of the saying and

the cross. Would that she had the power to obliterate the cruel words and add *Beloved Wife of Leah* to the stone. As Leah had said, where was their charity? How could love ever be wrong? Especially love as true as Sharla and Leah's had been.

She took a half-dozen photographs and then stood for a moment, wondering if she had anything she wanted to say. She suddenly felt foolish. She didn't believe Sharla was really there anymore. She'd never decided what she believed about an after-life, but her father had taught her to be open to all cultures and ideas. She sighed and looked up at the sky and thought that wherever Sharla was it had to be closer to Leah than this place.

She shook her head at herself, took one last picture, pinched a petal of each flower for her pockets and then went back to the car. On the drive back she composed and recomposed the note to Leah to include with the pictures. She would include the flower petals, so Leah could see the colors. She hadn't made this trip to get a response from Leah, but she hoped that Leah would respond and that she would see her again.

When she got to the hotel she surprised her mother with a long, heartfelt hug and tickets to a highly recommended live jazz club.

♥ ♥ ♥ ♥ ♥

"So what did you want to show us, Lee?" Valentina took another bite of her amaretto cheesecake and made delicate smacking sounds as though she were tasting wine. "Do you think this could use a little less amaretto?"

"Dearest, it's fine," Maureen said. "I don't see how a quarter teaspoon more or less of something would make a difference."

Valentina looked at her mate disdainfully. "You have no palate to speak of."

"I like the way you taste," Maureen said.

"Guys!" Leah looked at both her friends. "Let's not talk about sex."

Valentina pointed her fork at Leah. "Celibacy's a drag, isn't it? Believe me, I knew all about it until this one came along." She waved her fork at Maureen.

Leah chuckled. "It's not that bad unless your friends carry on in front of you."

"Sorry," Maureen said. "I'll be more circumspect." She opened her brown eyes very wide with an innocent air. "So what's with these pictures you said we had to see?"

Leah hmphed and said to Valentina, "A little less amaretto."

Valentina nodded. "Would you serve this with amaretto? Or would that be too much?" She pushed stray locks of her curly black hair back from her face.

"Lee." Maureen's voice held a bit of a whine.

"Too much. It's very sweet. I'm not sure what you'd serve. Something dry and sharp, maybe."

"Lee!" Maureen sat forward and imperiously held out her hand. "Show me the pictures."

Leah smiled indulgently at Maureen and handed over the packet of photos Jackie had included with her note. Valentina got up to look over Maureen's shoulder.

Both women caught their breath, then sighed.

Valentina crossed herself and looked up at Leah, her dark eyes shimmering with tears. "Did you finally have the heart to go looking for it? Did her family finally relent and let you know where she is?"

"No, I got them from a friend." Friend? Could she call Jackie merely a friend? The gesture she'd made by taking these photos — it went beyond that. "From an acquaintance, really." She gave them the brief highlights of Jackie's stay over Thanksgiving. Well, almost all the highlights. She left out the electric moments in the kitchen that last morning. She couldn't stop herself from thinking of the instant when her fingers had slid into Jackie's wetness. Her stomach lurched.

"What a sweet thing to do!" Maureen stared at the photographs. "And the flowers . . . Sharla would have loved them."

Leah gently poured the collection of petals onto the table. They had faded, but enough of the vibrant color remained for her to easily picture the way the bouquet had looked.

"Oh, Lee," Valentina said softly. "What a lovely person Jackie must be."

She nodded and closed her eyes briefly. Her throat was suddenly tight again. The photographs were beautifully composed. Jackie had sent directions on how she could find Sharla's grave — maybe she would go one day, but she didn't need to. Not anymore.

"Those bastards," Maureen said with some heat after reading Jackie's note. "How could they put that on her marker?"

"Same old story," Valentina said. "They don't see her for fifteen years and suddenly they have the legal right to her body and what money she had, and her car. Thank goodness you put both houses in your name, Lee. They'd have taken them, too. How they can call themselves Christian . . ." She lifted her gaze heavenward for a moment, then quickly crossed herself again. "I could wish them ill, I really could."

Leah shrugged. "I shouldn't have told them she died. I told them because it was the 'Christian' thing to do. And we see where that got me."

"Irony's a drag, isn't it?" Valentina returned to her seat and had another bite of cheesecake.

"What you should have done," Maureen said, "was make out wills. And durable powers of attorney. Val and I did that after they took Sharla away from you."

"Wills can be contested," Leah said. "Raymond Burr's family held it up forever and you'd think he knew enough to get good legal advice."

"It's better than nothing," Maureen said.

Leah picked up her favorite photograph. Taken low to the ground, the flowers framed the lower foreground, with Sharla's name behind them. Above the top of the marker blurry green branches mixed with gray light. Jackie had her mother's eye for balance. "You're right." She cleared her throat. "Would you like to keep one of the pictures?"

"Yes, if you don't mind," Maureen said. "Sharla was a good friend."

"Do you think I could serve a port with this cheesecake?" Valentina took another bite.

Maureen threw her napkin at Valentina.

Leah carefully swept the petals back into the envelope and gathered the photos. "I wouldn't know unless I tried it," she said.

Valentina's eyes lighted up. "What a good idea." She disappeared into the kitchen.

♥ ♥ ♥ ♥ ♥

"Last item," Angela said. "I've got two tickets to a benefit for the Women's Cancer Resource Center. It's an art gallery opening this Friday, but I can't use them. Anyone want to go?"

Jackie opened her mouth to say yes but thought she should let the partners have first crack at them.

"I'll take one," Diane said. "Mark won't want to go, so someone else should take the other one."

"I'd love it," Jackie said after no one else spoke up. "Thanks very much." The ticket was passed down the conference table to her and she tucked it in her calendar.

"I didn't know you were an art hound," Diane said as they left the conference room.

"Can't keep me away. Not that I can afford to buy anything." She didn't mention that she had a small, original Jellica Frakes sculpture in her apartment. Her mother had given it to her when she had left for college saying that, in her most practical motherly way, Jackie could always raise some cash on it if she needed to.

"That makes two of us. Why don't you grab the Dearborn file and we'll go over the new specs they sent and pick out somewhere to eat before the opening."

Jackie fetched the file Diane wanted from her shoebox-sized office — no bigger than her cubicle at L&B, but it had walls and a door — and walked the length of the office suite to Diane's office.

Diane looked up and said, "I was just thinking. I shouldn't have assumed you didn't have someone you'd like to take to the gallery opening. You could have the other ticket. I wouldn't mind."

"No, keep it," Jackie protested. "I'm very single at the moment." She thought of Leah and pushed away her hurt that she hadn't heard from Leah about the photos. She hoped that they hadn't gotten lost in the mail.

"Are you?" Diane considered her with her head tipped to one side. "Well, I have a friend who's a banker here in the city, and I think you'd get along great. Maybe I should give my ticket —"

"You don't have to," Jackie said. She felt her color rising. "I'm ... I mean, I do want to meet new people, but ..." She looked at her feet. Diane was nice and probably had nice friends. "Is your friend ... a man or a woman?"

"A woman," Diane said. "Oh dear, have I got it wrong?" She dropped her voice. "I know some nice men, too. Mark's brother, for instance, is a sweetheart. Nicer even than Mark but not as funny."

Jackie laughed with relief. "No, you got it right. I didn't know that you knew. I mean, I haven't known for that long." She frowned. "How *did* you know?"

Diane shrugged. "I don't — oh. Now I remember. Another friend of mine said she'd met someone whose name she couldn't remember at a dance, but it was someone who worked here and was new. I assumed it was you from her description. And since she's gay, I assumed you were, too. She said you're a great dancer."

It was Jackie's turn to blink. "Oh, that explains

it. I've been to a couple of women's dances, but it's hard to hear names over the music, much less remember them."

"Well," Diane said, "I could give my ticket to my banker friend and tell her I can't go and someone I work with is going, you could just gab about art and if you didn't like each other, you wouldn't have to stress about it, you wouldn't even have to talk to each other, and it wouldn't be a date, so what do you say?" She wiggled her eyebrows encouragingly.

"I'd wouldn't mind going with you," Jackie said. Diane continued to make encouraging faces until Jackie laughed. "But if your banker friend is really that nice, I guess I could live if she went in your place." She resolutely would not keep her evenings free for a mythical call from Leah that would never come.

"I'll call her this morning and see," Diane said, with a grin. "Back to business. The Dearborns have completely revised their dining hall ideas. Again. This is going to be the longest inn renovation on record. So guess what I need you to do?"

Jackie held out her hand for the specification sheet. "Blueprints and elevations with HVAC. Consider it done."

♥ ♥ ♥ ♥ ♥

"We only have to stay a few minutes, then maybe we can go dancing," Constance said.

"Maybe this won't be as dreary as the last one," Leah said. "Openings can be fun. I've been to a few that were. Well, at least one."

"*Painted Moon* will be an opening to remember, darling. I'm working on getting the Sunday magazine to do a photo spread."

"I'll do the installation as soon as you're ready for it." Leah opened the door for Constance who swept by her with the click of high heels and a waft of Chanel Number 19. She was wearing the same dress she always wore to gallery openings — a skin-tight sheath that closely matched her skin tone and was painted with sequins in all the right places. An expensive fake fur dangled over one shoulder and cabuchon-cut amber dangled from her ears.

Leah followed her in more sedate black slacks and deep purple jacket — her standard festive wear. As they approached the gallery owner for the obligatory handshake and well-wishes, she whispered in Constance's ear, "We can't go dancing with you in that get-up. You'll split a seam."

Constance wrinkled her nose. "You're probably right. We could go back to my place, though. I could change. Or not." She threw a wicked smile over her shoulder.

"Connie . . ." Lee began wearily. She broke off to add her smile and "Good luck," to the owner. Even though she and Constance had agreed to be friends only, Constance still flirted with her and Leah was bothered by the mixed signals. Then they were past the receiving line and into the main gallery which was primarily occupied by sculpture.

A few pieces immediately caught Lee's eye. Constance was already deep into the room, making a beeline for a photographer Lee remembered vaguely from an exhibit several years ago. Constance must have seen something she liked — Lee recognized the signs. Photographs would be displayed in Constance's gallery, eventually.

She drifted to the exhibits that intrigued her. The gallery was filling up — definitely a success. Constance began working the crowd, something she was very good at. Leah watched her for a while, in between studying the pieces.

She came to a Jellica Frakes piece, one she hadn't seen. Oh, it was lovely — made her fingers itch. It was cast wrought iron painted white, and about four inches in diameter at the base, flowing upward about six feet to a breadth of about three feet. At the top the iron curved over and spilled downward again. The downward slope was a replica of fine lace work. In fact, it was very like a long bridal train upside down. The lace work was delicate-looking but the piece itself, Leah thought, was about deceptive strength.

She stepped back to admire it further and trod on someone's foot. The owner of the foot squawked. She spun around to apologize. "I'm so sorry —"

She was face to face with Jackie.

Jackie's annoyed expression melted into shock. They stared at each other.

Leah had not forgotten the blue of Jackie's eyes. She had not forgotten the way her lips were shaped, or how they parted when Jackie was breathing hard.

Jackie was breathing hard.

Leah realized she was breathing hard, too. It had only taken this glance to put her right back in the kitchen at the cabin and recreate the same feelings in her body she had had then. The texture of Jackie's skin. The taste of her lips.

"I take it you two have met," a voice said.

Leah blinked. Jackie took a deep breath like a

swimmer coming up for air. Her gaze fell away and she glanced at the petite woman in a business suit who stood next to her.

"Umm, Leah this is Laurel, a friend of a friend. Laurel, this is Lee Beck, the artist."

"Pleased to meet you," Laurel murmured. A smile hovered around her mouth. "I see a . . . piece over there I want to study, so I'll catch you later, Jackie. If I don't, say hi to Diane for me, okay?"

Jackie opened her mouth as though she wanted to ask Laurel to stay, but then merely nodded. Laurel melted into the crowd, but not before she looked at both of them again with raised eyebrows and a knowing smile.

"I got the pictures," Leah said. "I don't know how to thank you. I've picked up the phone once a day and words . . . words failed me."

"It was nothing."

"It was more than nothing."

"I mean I was glad to do it. And you're welcome." Jackie was staring at the floor and Leah couldn't stand it.

"Look at me."

Jackie looked up and their gazes locked again. Her lips were slightly parted and they trembled slightly. Leah glanced down at the turquoise silk blouse she wore, and the short black skirt. This was the everyday Jackie, not the woman who had been stranded at her cabin in Sharla's clothes. The everyday Jackie overwhelmed Leah's nerves even more than the snowbound Jackie had. Leah had not thought it possible.

Their intense stare was broken by someone jostling Leah into Jackie. She felt the warmth of

Jackie's silk-clad breasts against her and every nerve ignited.

"It's so crowded in here," she said weakly. "Maybe we can find a place to talk."

"Talk," Jackie echoed. Leah took her by the arm and led the way to the back of the gallery. There had to be somewhere with a little privacy. She found an unlocked door at the end of a side room and propelled Jackie through it. Crates and packing materials left little floor space, so they stood behind the closed door.

She turned Jackie to face her and lost all her resolve. She had wanted to be alone with Jackie and now she was. The sight of Jackie's face looking up at her — those trembling lips. She looked so vulnerable Leah was afraid to touch her. If she touched her she wasn't sure she would be able to stop again.

It was Jackie who slowly raised her hand. She slid her finger under the lapel of Leah's jacket. "Nice jacket," she said in a faint voice, as though she was trying to make normal conversation but her composure had failed her.

Her fingers slipped downward and released Leah's jacket. Leah caught her hand and then the distance between them was gone in a breathless moment of arms winding and bodies arching. The silk covering Jackie's back was warm and only enhanced the softness of the skin underneath. Her braid was heavy against Leah's hands. It would be so easy to slide the blouse to one side and feast on the warmth of Jackie's shoulders. She kissed the exposed curve of Jackie's throat. Jackie's breath was an indrawn hiss echoed by a tremor in her body as she pulled Leah's head down.

Leah clung to her desperately, her every intention to finish what they had begun in her kitchen. A half-step backward put Jackie's shoulders against the door. Jackie moaned through their pressed lips, arching her full breasts against Leah. Her arms dropped to Leah's waist, sliding under her jacket.

Leah's hands were under Jackie's skirt, caressing the smooth hips through thin pantyhose. Still she kissed Jackie, her tongue exploring the welcoming mouth, inviting exploration in return.

Jackie's knees buckled and only the pressure of Leah against her kept her from sliding to the floor. Leah slipped her leg between Jackie's, suddenly aware that they were reaching a point of no return in a semi-public place.

She broke their kiss, leaving Jackie gasping. "I want to be with you," she murmured in Jackie's ear. "I mean it. But not here."

Jackie turned her head to one side. "I know. I want to." Her voice was barely audible. "I don't want you to stop. But I feel like I'm going to pass out. I want you to make love to me." She pressed her forehead into Leah's shoulder.

Leah held her until Jackie stood up on her own and raised her head. "It's overwhelming," she whispered. "Nothing else matters."

"I know," Leah said. She smiled and traced the corner of Jackie's mouth with her thumb.

"You don't know," Jackie said, suddenly vehement. "You can still stand up. You are still . . . intact."

Leah feathered a kiss over one eyebrow. "I don't feel intact."

"But you are," Jackie said. "I'm in pieces." She drew a deep breath. "I . . . I'm not a weak person. I'm self-reliant."

"I know," Leah said with another smile.

Jackie shook her head slightly. "Right now I would do whatever you told me to. I've never felt like this." Her voice dropped lower so that Leah had to listen carefully to catch every word. "I've never let go like this. If you told me I had to stand here while you — while you made love to me I'd find a way. I would do anything you asked of me. It doesn't seem like I have a choice anymore."

Leah shivered. She was frightened suddenly by the control Jackie was yielding to her. "I won't ask anything you can't give."

A tear escaped and trailed slowly down the curve of Jackie's cheek. "I don't want to be like this. Dependent and clinging. But I can't help it. I don't want to do it here either. But I can't let go of you." Her grip on Leah tightened and her voice quavered. "I can't let go. I'll fall to pieces if I do."

"I have hold of you," Leah said. "I'm not letting go."

They stood locked in each other's arms for a long time. Jackie finally took a deep breath and stood a little straighter. "I don't feel so lightheaded any more."

"Do you want to leave?"

Jackie nodded.

No one noticed their emergence from the room, probably because the gallery was even more packed than before. Leah linked her arm with Jackie's, aware that Jackie was pressing close beside her. She felt like a salmon swimming upstream. As they entered the main room of the gallery it seemed everyone suddenly knew Leah and wanted to talk.

Jackie said very little and Leah could tell every word was an effort. They were two-thirds of the way to the door when Constance materialized.

"Lee?" She put her hand on Lee's arm and glanced at Jackie. "What's up, darling?"

Leah felt Jackie's withdrawal. She tightened her grip on Jackie's arm and said to Constance, "I have to leave, okay?"

Constance looked again at Jackie, a long, considering stare. "I thought we had a date."

"I know. I'm sorry. I don't want to leave you in the lurch, but —"

"You're going to anyway. Thanks a lot, darling," Constance said. Her smile didn't go any further than her mouth. She leaned closer to Leah. "Would you introduce me to the woman you're dumping me for?"

Jackie came to life and said quietly, "I'm Jackie Frakes. I met Leah last Thanksgiving."

"Jackie." Constance echoed. She looked at Leah and Leah could see the anger building in Constance's eyes.

"I was honest with you, Connie."

"Do you think that matters right now? Speaking of honesty, I thought she was straight."

Leah was at a loss. She had forgotten about Parker.

Jackie's voice, still quiet, fell into the silence. "Not anymore. I'm a lesbian."

Constance took a step back, looking as stunned as Leah felt. She smiled bitterly at Leah. "Congratulations on converting someone to the faith, darling."

She dropped her voice. "I'm sorry, I don't mean to be a bitch, but Lee, you don't need some neophyte mucking up your life. You just got it together."

"I know what I want," Leah said.

Constance locked gazes with her. "You always have, haven't you?" Then she turned and walked away.

11

Jackie felt as though she was walking under water. At Leah's prompting she gave the cab driver her address. She sat in the darkness aware of the heat from Leah's body, aware of the smell of her shampoo and the faint odor of dry cleaning solution that clung to her jacket.

Her senses were overloaded. She could hear the steady pace of Leah's breathing, the rumble of the cab's engine and the beating of her own heart.

Leah took her hand and the rhythm of her pulse

deafened all other sounds. Her eyes only faintly saw the passing street lights.

"Is this it?" Leah's voice seemed to come from far away.

Jackie looked at the house and after a moment was able to say huskily, "Yes, this is it."

She gave her keys to Leah at the front door and then led the way up the arduous three flights to her apartment. Leah unlocked the door after Jackie pointed out the right key and she led the way inside, stopping just inside the door, her legs trembling.

Leah shut the door and the room plunged into darkness.

Jackie closed her eyes, awash with vertigo. Her breath caught in her throat and she told herself as fiercely as she could manage that she could not cry.

"Jackie, what's wrong?" Softly out of the dark, Leah turned Jackie and wrapped her arms around her.

"I'm scared," Jackie said. "I want you so badly I'm scaring myself."

Leah kissed her softly. "I don't mean to frighten you." She gasped slightly. "I won't hurt you. I couldn't."

"I'm not afraid of you," Jackie whispered. She was afraid of herself, she wanted to say, but the words wouldn't form. She had thought she was ready. But she realized she might not recognize herself in the morning.

It had all seemed so rational, intellectual even. But it wasn't. There was nothing rational about her desire. The consciousness of choice had left her the moment that she looked into Leah's eyes again.

She slid her hands under Leah's jacket and pushed it off Leah's shoulders, then she fumbled with the first button on Leah's shirt, but it wouldn't come undone. She gave a sob of frustration.

Leah captured her fingers and said quietly, "Why don't you sit down on the bed?"

Jackie nodded and walked backward to the bed, her hands gripping Leah's. Her eyes were adjusting to the darkness and she could see Leah's gentle expression.

She sat down and looked up at Leah. Her fingers went to the buttons of Leah's shirt again, but she had no better success. Her mind was lost in a haze. She rested her forehead on Leah's stomach and fought back tears.

Leah tipped Jackie's head up, then knelt in front of her. She kissed Jackie with the lightest of touches.

"Help me," Jackie said. Her arms were too heavy to lift, her legs ached. "Please."

Leah's fingers were more certain with Jackie's buttons and she slowly pulled the silk blouse open and carefully reached around to unhook Jackie's bra.

Jackie shrugged the blouse down her shoulders and impatiently pulled her bra down.

"You're getting tangled," Leah started to say, but Jackie pulled her head down, bringing Leah's mouth to her breasts.

"Dear God," Jackie murmured. She inched back on the bed and Leah's mouth followed her hungrily, then Leah was kneeling over her, feasting on Jackie's breasts even as Jackie crushed Leah's mouth to her.

Jackie wrapped her legs around one of Leah's, bringing herself urgently against Leah's hips. Her own passion was frightening. She couldn't stop herself to wonder if Leah felt the same desperate need. She worried that her desire would repulse Leah, but she couldn't slow down. Her mind told her that she didn't know what to do, but her body knew. Her hands went to Leah's shirt again and when the buttons wouldn't give way she tore them.

Leah groaned and her mouth left Jackie's breasts. She stood up for only a moment, shaking off her torn shirt, and kicking off her slacks. Then she was kneeling over Jackie again.

She rolled Jackie over, unbuttoned and unzipped her skirt, then rolled her face up again. Jackie was dizzy. She didn't care, just lifted her hips so Leah could pull her skirt down. She heard her pantyhose shred and then her clothes hitting the floor. She opened her legs and grabbed Leah's hand and guided it to the burning heat.

Her own groan drowned out Leah's. She had never been this wet and this ready. "Show me," she said hoarsely. "Show me what it's like between women."

Her body was rigid with sensation; only her hips felt like liquid, rippling in response to the strength of Leah's fingers. Leah murmured something incoherent as Jackie lifted her hips to meet her. Her body was an aching blur soothed by Leah's fingers inside her, quicker now, harder now.

Something would explode, she had no idea what. She couldn't stand this pleasure — it was almost agony. She writhed to meet Leah, heard Leah murmuring in her passion and then knew — she was exploding with deep, wrenching moans, frighteningly primal, sounds she'd never made before. Her body spasmed, her lungs felt as though they would burst.

She crested at a peak she hadn't even dreamed could be so incredibly high. She sank sobbing for air into the bed, Leah's fingers deep within her. She felt, with a tremor that left her muscles aching, Leah's tongue on her.

Her whole body was liquid now. Leah's tongue swept through her, into her. Jackie whimpered as Leah's fingers left her, then sighed as Leah wrapped her arms tightly around her hips, crushing Jackie's wetness to her mouth. Jackie melted into the bed, her body a river of sensation, seeking equilibrium. She was at peace for a moment, then Leah's tongue flickered over the tender nerves between her legs and Jackie began the long climb to ecstasy again, unsure she could rise that high again, not a second time. But Leah's mouth drove her higher, lifted her to a new peak.

The air was thin, her head spun, but she was anchored to reality by Leah's tongue on her. She grabbed Leah's hands, held them bruisingly tight as she surged against Leah's mouth. She came in a moment of perfect stillness, her muscles balanced against Leah's, eyes clenched to purple fireworks. Then Leah released her hands and Jackie let her head fall back. Her legs slid limply down onto Leah's shoulders and she rested, sublimely aware of her breath filling her lungs and the silk of Leah's hair on her thigh.

Leah shivered as the fine film of perspiration on her back chilled. Sharla had never needed her like that. Constance had been needy, but self-contained at all times. And they had been all she had known, until now. Until Jackie brought her almost to the point of tears.

She wanted to concentrate on Jackie, but Sharla crowded in — how could she help but think of her? Was it wrong to compare them? She and Sharla had developed their sexual communication gradually, finding in each other the needs that shaped their passion. It had been several years before the sex was staggeringly powerful, but that had been different from what she felt now, her fingers and face covered with Jackie's scent. Right now she was scared she had gone too far and too fast for her, but Jackie had stunned Leah with the powerful contractions of her body, pulling Leah in, asking for more until Leah wasn't sure she could keep up.

She was exhausted and could have slept, leaving the moment of having Jackie perfect unto itself. Her body reminded her of her own needs and she quelled them, not sure what Jackie would be ready to do. Jackie seemed to be asleep.

Then Jackie stirred with a long, deep sigh. "Thank you for that," she said, her voice drifting softly down around Leah's ears. "So that's what I've been missing."

"I'm sorry I was mean that morning —"

"Don't be! Oh God, don't be."

Leah wanted to admit that she wasn't a vastly experienced lover and that she was feeling brand new sensations. And that she was scared. Should she tell Jackie that she wanted to bury her face between Jackie's thighs again and stay there, that she wanted in the worst way to feel Jackie's fingers inside her, that she was ready to give all control to Jackie in the same degree Jackie had given it to her? Too soon. It was too far to jump.

Fear made her cautious and she tried for a joking tone. "Have you got it out of your system?"

Jackie was quiet and then she reached for Leah's hand, drawing the coated fingers to her mouth. Her tongue slowly traced a line up Leah's palm and index finger, then she put Leah's hand on her breast. "I want it in my system for always."

Leah trembled as Jackie's hips moved in a tiny circle, echoing the rhythm of Leah's hand stroking her breast. She closed her eyes and inhaled Jackie's scent, then Jackie sat up and pushed Leah onto her back.

She took Leah in her arms with a deep, sensuous kiss. One hand played over Leah's breasts, then her lips left Leah's mouth to tease the small, erect tips. Leah felt the caresses in every nerve, crowding out all other sensation. She almost didn't hear Jackie's whispered question.

"Is this okay?"

"Yes," Leah murmured. She looked down and felt a rush of passion at the sight of Jackie's mouth on her breasts. "I like that."

Jackie raised her head slightly. "You'll tell me, won't you? If I do something you don't like?"

Leah nodded, unable to speak, then she pulled Jackie's head down to her breasts again. She closed her eyes and arched her back and let the exquisite teasing apply layer after layer of passion to her trembling body. Jackie's mouth became demanding, her caresses frantic and Leah's hips jerked in response.

Jackie raised her head again and Leah looked

down, met her burning gaze. "Is it okay?" She licked her lips. "Can I . . . I want to . . ." Her glance flickered down Leah's body.

Leah pushed herself up on one elbow and ran one hand over Jackie's hair, tracing the ripples where the braiding began. Her hand cupped Jackie's neck as Jackie kissed her thigh. Gently, she pressed Jackie's head toward her, trying to say without words that she wanted Jackie to taste her.

Jackie nodded slightly, her eyes closed. Leah watched Jackie lower her mouth to her and heard Jackie's hungry groan. Her vision swam at the sight of Jackie's beautiful body curved over her own, the pale cream of Jackie's throat against the darker tint of her own thighs. Her arms gave out, she fell back and felt Jackie gather her more fiercely into her arms.

Jackie began gently, but with a sure touch that deepened. She shifted her position and held Leah open, her tongue exploring folds and ripples, then sinking into the font of Leah's wetness. She teased until Leah was thrusting her hips up and moaning and then her mouth sank deeply into Leah's flesh, holding Leah to her with crushing strength. Leah bucked, stifling the cry that was building in her chest. She felt Jackie's hips jerk in response as Leah's body tensed once, twice and a third time with enough force to break Jackie's grip and paint the back of Leah's eyelids with crimson lightning.

She wasn't prepared for the soft glide of Jackie's fingers into her. She moaned. "I can't."

Jackie whispered, "I want to taste you again. While I do this to you." Her fingers moved slowly and her tongue was the lightest caress.

"I don't think I can. I...one's usually enough...." Leah tried to roll on her side, but Jackie pinned Leah's weak, trembling legs easily. Leah relented, too weak to struggle and not wanting to disappoint her.

"I'll go slow," Jackie said. Her tongue whispered over Leah again, her fingers moved languidly. "Just let me taste you and feel you."

Leah raised herself to look at Jackie again. Jackie's eyes were closed, her concentration seemingly devoted to the feel of Leah around her fingers and the taste of Leah on her tongue. Her expression was rapturous, ravenous — Leah flooded with desire again. And saw Jackie pause, become aware of the welcome of Leah's new wetness.

Jackie smiled with sensuous success and her touch grew firmer.

Leah gave herself up to Jackie's gentle demands and found, to her wonder, that she could respond again, not as fiercely, but this time with a complete awareness of each place Jackie touched her and Jackie's unmistakable pleasure.

♥ ♥ ♥ ♥ ♥

Jackie pulled the bedclothes over them, what she could find, anyway. Nothing was anchored anymore. "Are you comfortable?" To her own ears, her voice was different. Less breathy, a little deeper in pitch. Adult.

Leah's hips shifted toward her. "I'm fine. Very comfortable."

Jackie let her arm fall across Leah's ribs again and she lightly kissed Leah's back. "Me, too."

She slid into a light sleep where she had just enough control to direct her thoughts to the past hours. To relive the intense moments and feel the lassitude of satisfaction seep through her body again. Utterly satisfied, yet invigorated. She felt, under her fatigue, as though she could run a marathon with brand new muscles and stamina. She felt as if she had finally discovered the strength of her own body and what she was capable of feeling and giving.

Surprising, she mused as she drifted to sleep. Strength from loving a woman. She smiled into Leah's soft shoulder. Was it the love or the woman, she wondered. Or both?

12

"What's your favorite color?" Leah pulled gently on Jackie's earlobe and memorized the soft pink.

Jackie stretched her arms in the morning sunlight and rolled over to face Leah. "The lavender of African violets. And flag red." She smiled impishly. "What's your favorite book?"

"*Nature*. It's Emerson. What's your favorite food?"

"Crème brulée with blueberries. What's your favorite kind of music?"

"Jazz, when it's live."

"Yeah?" Jackie plumped up her pillow and grinned. "Me too."

They traded insights into their private likes and dislikes while Leah decided what mixture of paints would match the color of Jackie's eyes. Blue alone wouldn't do it. A dash of black and a startling ring of yellow.

An hour passed in talk and laughter. Leah felt more at ease with Jackie than she had at the cabin.

A door slammed downstairs, breaking their comfortable cocoon. Leah didn't want to acknowledge the passage of time, but it was inevitable. She sat up and her stomach growled.

"That's a hint, I think," Jackie said. "I can make coffee and toaster biscuits, if you like." Jackie wrapped a sheet around her body and padded to the little kitchen area. "I'll turn on the heater, too."

"I'd like that very much." Leah watched the thick braid sway against the white of the sheet as Jackie walked away from her. She glanced around the tiny apartment with pleased chagrin. The blankets and comforter were tangled, in marked contrast to tidy bookshelves, a coffee table with what had to be a Jellica Frakes sculpture, and the bright, clear lines of a large Jasper Johns print. Their clothes were strewn from the doorway to the bed. She caught sight of her shirt with its torn buttons and a tingle of new want made her tremble. It wouldn't take much to be ready again for Jackie's touch and her kisses.

She closed her eyes and unexpectedly she saw Sharla's haunting face illuminated with passion, heard her murmuring that Leah was her goddess, that there could never be anyone else. They had pledged each other their faith and loyalty forever. She trembled again, this time from a chill that bit into the pit of her stomach.

Leah wrapped herself in a blanket and stumbled to the bathroom. In the shower she ran the water as hot as she could stand and scrubbed herself vigorously, trying to drown out memories of Sharla.

They had never talked about what they would want a survivor to do. She knew that Sharla would not have wanted her to be alone. She was — had been — too generous. So why did she feel disloyal now? When she hadn't with Constance?

"I don't love Sharla less. I never will," she said to the shampoo bottle. A dancing ache started in her stomach. Was is possible to have loved someone as much as she had Sharla and find a new place in her heart with as much depth and feeling for Jackie? Did she really deserve such love twice in one lifetime? It was more likely that she was missing coupledom. What she had had with Sharla had been lasting and true. She didn't want to give or receive anything less than that. It wasn't in her nature.

She asked herself if she had a whole heart to offer Jackie.

Yes, it was possible. But she wasn't *in* love. Falling in love with Jackie would be a selfish thing to do. Jackie was nine or so years younger than she was, and younger than that in lesbian years. Attractive and fun and intelligent and caring, Jackie could have her choice of anyone, while she herself had already had a lifetime of love with Sharla. That Jackie had needed to have sex was evident — but that was just closure on what they had started over Thanksgiving.

No doubt Jackie would be ready to play the field now and experience what being a lesbian in San Francisco had to offer. She would not stand in her way.

She combed her hair and repeated her resolve. She would make no demands. She wasn't in love.

When she saw Jackie sitting on the bed, unbraiding her hair, with the sheet revealing the delicate curve of her spine, she felt her body flinch from the onslaught of desire.

Jackie looked up and smiled, then clutched the sheet modestly around her as she went into the bathroom.

Leah poured herself coffee and listened to the thrum of the shower, then the hair dryer. When Jackie opened the bathroom door she was wearing a white robe and holding masses of her hair to the mouth of the dryer.

"This will take another ten minutes or so," she said. "I often think of having it cut."

"Don't," Leah said. "It's too beautiful."

"It's heavy and unruly," Jackie said, swirling most of it up onto her head and drying her scalp. "I have to braid it or it's constantly snarled. It takes forever to do your own French braid, too."

"It's still beautiful," Leah said, smiling.

Jackie smiled back and Leah retreated to the bed, wondering if she should get dressed. She really should. She would not stake any claims for Jackie by staying with her through the day — another night. Her breasts tightened with a sudden ache.

She sipped her coffee and calmed herself. Tried to, at least. She focused on the prosaic and picked up her torn shirt. Behind her, the hair dryer stopped.

"I'm sorry about that," Jackie said, crossing the room. "A waste of good cloth."

Leah returned Jackie's smile. "Don't be."

"I couldn't get the buttons undone and I couldn't wait," Jackie said shyly. She sat down on the bed. "I could tell you didn't have a bra on ... I'm ... I've never been in such a hurry before."

"I don't really need a bra. Not like you."

A delicate pink swelled up Jackie's throat. "You're ... there's enough to enjoy." She slowly slid her hands under the blanket and cupped Leah's breasts. Leah heard Jackie's breath catch, perhaps surprised to find her so erect.

"I love the way your body feels," Jackie said. The color in her face deepened. "And the way it makes my body feel."

Leah shivered and hot coffee splashed onto the bed. She swore mildly and got up, dabbing at the spill with the blanket.

"It's okay, it was only a little," Jackie said. "Put the cup down."

Leah looked at Jackie, knowing if she let go of the coffee cup all her resolutions would go up in a puff of passion.

"Put it down," Jackie said again, her voice more forceful. "Come back to bed." She rose to her knees and untied her robe, letting it slide down her body. Her breasts were points of carnation pink through the thick curls of her unbraided hair. She shrugged her hair impatiently over her shoulders and Leah swayed, recalling how Jackie's breasts tasted when they were as aroused as they had been last night.

Desperate desire was crowding out good sense. She told herself that Jackie needed her freedom or else she'd always wonder about what she hadn't explored. Jackie was just getting her out of her system, to be able to go on to women who could offer her an undamaged heart and a fresh spirit. And what about Sharla, she asked herself. She needed to think it through. Certainly she could put aside her own throbbing needs — good God, had she ever wanted Sharla like this? Yes, but at the moment it didn't seem possible. She flushed and her composure wavered in a tangle of guilt and passion.

"Is something wrong?" Jackie pulled her robe back to her shoulders and stepped off the bed. She put her arms around Leah's waist. "What are you thinking about?"

"Sharla." She stopped. She could have bitten her tongue off.

Jackie went pale and stood stock still for a moment, then she wrapped the robe tightly around her. "I'm sorry. I forgot." She went into the kitchen and poured herself coffee, her manner brisk.

Leah stood there miserably for a moment. You fool, she cursed herself. You, stupid, stupid fool.

"I'm afraid I'll need to borrow a T-shirt," Leah said before her throat completely seized up. Why had she brought Sharla into it? How could she have been so cruel again — what had she expected Jackie to do? Everything had turned into a mushy, ugly gray. All the contrasts were gone. No light, no shadow. She clenched her eyes for a moment and saw nothing.

When she opened them, Jackie was the picture of composure. She had found Leah a shirt and when she handed it to her, a lock of soft, curling hair trailed over Leah's wrist. It was heavy, like sewing silks. Leah wanted to feel that hair sweeping over her

163

body, to wallow in the sensuous delight of it in her hands. She envisioned herself on her back, Jackie's hair spread over her thighs, Jackie's mouth on her.

Jackie didn't say anything, which was just as well. Leah couldn't have spoken except to beg Jackie to take her to bed. But it was too late for begging and she was too proud. She had begged God to bring Sharla back. God hadn't answered. Sharla had stayed dead. Sharla . . .

She gathered her clothes and shakily dressed in the bathroom. Jackie said she had called a taxi for Leah. Leah took the dismissal in stride. She'd asked for it. She promised to call.

Later, she was amazed that her legs supported her down the three flights of stairs.

♥ ♥ ♥ ♥ ♥

By kneeling on the dresser, Jackie could see down into the street. She waited until the cab came and went, then she sank down onto the ball of linens and bedspread and let the tears leak out of her tightly closed eyes.

She found herself crying like she had never cried before. She tried to chide herself out of it, reminding herself that her life wasn't over, there were plenty of women who weren't recovering from the death of their only love. She wanted to hate Sharla for having ruined Leah for anyone else, but Sharla wasn't the one who had hurt her — Leah had.

Maybe it was one of those things — a quick flare of passion that was over for both of them. But that was a lie, on her part at least. She had ached to go to bed with Leah again, offered and been refused. Had she been too bold? She had never done that before, tried to initiate sex. Parker had always been the one to start things, as had her first boyfriend. But she had wanted to let Leah know how she felt. That she wanted to spend the day with Leah, talk, go out, begin a life together. For a brief hour she had been invincible, secure in the power of her love of women, of this woman.

Her body was hot from her crying and memories of how bold she had been by telling Leah what she wanted to do last night. She'd believed she could sense what Leah wanted. She flushed as she recalled teasing Leah, making her wait, but Leah had responded. Jackie couldn't have mistaken the signs. She'd had so few lovers — had Leah found her inexpert? Worse yet, was she just a novelty? A way to forget about Sharla?

She knew the last thoughts were unworthy of Leah, but then again, what did she know? And who was that woman at the gallery? Someone else Leah was using to get over Sharla?

So she had let Leah know she still wanted her. And Leah hadn't wanted her back. Fine. She sat up and wiped her face. She would bear it somehow. There were plenty of other women in San Francisco. She'd been around the goddamned world. It would take more than Leah Beck to set her back.

She bathed her face and threw herself into making the bed with fresh sheets, doing laundry, walking to the grocery store, getting some bagels and cream cheese from the deli and a pint of extra dark chocolate ice cream. She told herself all through the day that she was doing fine and would manage without Leah in her life. Her mental cheerleader worked overtime.

At home again, she looked at the events calendar. There was a Motown dance put on by the career women's group the Saturday after next. She had some stiff deadlines and demanding drawings to complete at work so a dance to look forward to would keep her going. And maybe she'd meet a woman to make her forget about Leah Beck, and maybe she'd go home with her.

♥ ♥ ♥ ♥ ♥

Leah picked up her car from in front of Constance's house, knowing she should go in and apologize for leaving Connie to find her own way home last night. But speech was beyond her. Driving was almost more than she could manage.

At home she felt the echoes of the last time she had been in this kind of pain. Butch whined for food, and she automatically dished some out. Then she went into the bedroom, seized the bedspread, dragged it after her into the walk-in closet, turned off the light and shut the door. She crawled into the corner, wrapped herself in the blanket, and turned her face from the tiny crack of light framing the closet door.

She squeezed her eyes closed until there was no color. Just blackness to swamp her in misery. She was beyond tears, but not beyond pain. An image seared across her eyelids — Sharla, unconscious, slipping under the water. Orange stunned her mind's eye — the life jacket bobbed up, empty. She cried out and heard her voice disappear into the clothes over her head.

She was losing Sharla again. Waves of guilt wracked her lungs, mired her in a brackish green wasteland. She was in love with Jackie. She was certain. She loved Sharla — *had* loved Sharla.

Was it really in the past tense? Was that what was causing her such agony now? She *had* loved Sharla. Her mind posed unanswerable questions. If she had met Jackie while Sharla was alive, would she have loved her? If Sharla came back from the dead, who would she choose?

You don't have to choose, she told herself. You have loving Sharla to keep forever. All the memories, the passion, the laughter. Waking to each day with such joy. But now it seemed as if she had to lose a little of Sharla to love Jackie without reservation.

Blue and silver danced in her mind's eye and her aching shoulder muscles relaxed. She concentrated on breathing deeply for a few minutes.

More at peace, she smiled in the darkness and drew a mental picture of Jackie as she had been that morning, the sheet draped around her back.

Her back tensed as Jackie's face went gray. The intriguing face turned away as she drew back at the mention of Sharla. She had hurt Jackie deeply. Even if Jackie didn't return her love with the same depth, they had shared an incredible night together. She wanted to take back the words, but it was over. She was sure that Jackie was done with her forever.

Leah had shown her how it could be between women and now Jackie was free to explore with her adventurous spirit and joyful openness to life. She had expected nothing from her encounter with Jackie and that was exactly what she had ended up with. So why wasn't she happy?

Blue and silver streaks mingled in the tears that finally came.

Jackie paid the admission fee and picked her way through the bar so she could be closer to the dance floor. "My Girl" was playing and the lights were dimmed as couples swayed together. When the song ended and the lights went up again, "Rockin' Robin" came on and Jackie looked around for anyone she knew.

"Hey, I hoped you would be here," someone said in her ear. She turned and grinned at Stella, a favorite dancing partner, who seized her hand and pulled her onto the floor. Stella was tall, round, large and a good leader, especially for a swing beat. Jackie threw herself into enjoying the music and the dancing — she could forget about Leah.

"Go, girl," Stella called, handing Jackie in and out of two turns, a you go, I Go then into a sugar push. When the music ended they hugged and applauded. The D.J. put on "ABC" and Stella twirled her into a different swing step.

Several songs later Stella pushed her off the floor and led the way to the quietest corner of the club. Her lover, Bonnie, was talking to a woman Jackie had met once before. Stella dropped a breathless kiss on Bonnie's forehead and said, "Room for me?"

Bonnie pulled Stella onto the arm of her

wheelchair and smiled a welcome at Jackie. "You're good for her — she never gets this much exercise."

Jackie fanned herself. "And vice versa." She nodded hello to Ina.

Ina returned the hello with a mischievous grin. "Can I get you a beer? Or would you like to dance?" She inclined her blond brush-cut toward the dance floor.

"Yes to both," Jackie said promptly. Stella had told her, with heavy maternal overtones, that Ina was a fast worker. Maybe that was just what she needed. "Dance first?"

Ina followed her back to the dance floor where the D.J. had segued to "Surfin' U.S.A." Jackie showed Ina how to do the swim and backstroke. Ina nuzzled her ears when they slow danced to "Dock of the Bay." Jackie controlled the urge to squirm, all at once uncertain about her course of action. Maybe another woman wasn't the way to forget Leah. Not this soon.

To Jackie's relief, the D.J. declared a line dance and the floor cleared for the Electric Slide.

"How do you know this one?" Ina studied Jackie's steps.

" 'Soul Train.' When I was a kid they were crazy for 'Soul Train' in Spain. You can do it, it's simple." Ina caught on quickly and when the song ended they left the floor with their arms around each other's waist.

The beer was cold and Jackie felt a little more bold. She munched popcorn while Ina flirted with her and then went back to the dance floor for a long, slow dance to "Me and Mrs. Jones."

Ina nuzzled her ears again and Jackie forced herself to relax. The kiss wasn't so bad — pleasant even — and Jackie again tried to persuade herself that she was doing the right thing. Damn you, Leah Beck, she thought.

They sat out a set and Jackie spent most of it talking to Bonnie who was a library of information about anything to do with lesbians in San Francisco. She knew all the books, all the plays, all the gossip, all the art. Ina joined in a couple of times, but said that politics and activism were not her forte, nor were books or theater. She liked to dance. Her gaze, flickering over Jackie's body, said there were other things she liked.

I won't have anything to talk to her about, Jackie thought. She and Leah hadn't had that much time for talk, but they hadn't found any topics they weren't both interested in. But tonight is just for sex, she told herself. To get Leah out of her system. Ina clearly didn't expect anything else.

Even as she talked with Bonnie, Jackie puzzled over what to do. Just because her sexuality had been turned inside out, did that mean her sexual mores had as well? She hadn't been interested in casual sex when she had been with men, so why should she be now? It was probably safe and her days of worrying about birth control were over. But *probably* safe wasn't good enough. And her self-image was the most precious thing she possessed. She was angry at Leah Beck, and Ina didn't have anything to do with it.

She sighed. Her self-image had undergone enough change. So even if her body was interested in going to bed with Ina — which it didn't seem to be — her mind was not. Unlike the situation with Leah, she could choose to be with Ina.

At the thought of Leah, her body prickled and she felt lightheaded. Still ready for Leah's touch, but no other. The hurt was there, too.

"Are you feeling okay?" Bonnie gently shook her arm.

Jackie started, then looked at Ina. As good an excuse as any, she thought. "No, not really. I suddenly feel very weak."

"I can drive you home," Ina offered.

Jackie stood up shakily, cursing herself. Just thinking about going to bed with Leah left her drained. It wasn't fair. "No, I'll be fine. I had a really long week at work and not much sleep. I suppose it's catching up with me." She smiled to allay Bonnie's obvious concern. "I'd better go now."

Ina looked resigned and she was already eyeing the dance floor for another partner. Jackie made her goodbyes and walked to her car. The snapping wind cleared her mind and even as she drove away she kicked herself. So much for being seductive and seducible.

Damn you, Leah Beck, and the snowstorm you rode in on.

13

At the edge of her hearing, Leah knew the phone was ringing again. She continued to ignore it. Every ounce of energy she had was directed at finishing the five canvases she was working on simultaneously.

Today was rubine red for depth and to give translucency to the creamy figure that would be painted over it. Her back was killing her but she remained bent over the first canvas, working laboriously with a wide tipped brush. Here would be a knee and the inner curve of thigh. The canvas immediately to the right already had the outline of the same shapely leg, but smaller. It was topped by round, voluptuous hips. Hips that looked as though they would move like a dancer's.

In the third canvas she used more red where eventually a breast would emerge, along with the arm, shoulder and stomach of the same woman. A woman she could paint a thousand times from memory now. A thick braid of hair dangled from the open curve of the body and there Leah intended to use braided blackened pewter tied with a ribbon of bronze.

In the fourth canvas, a long line dominated, taking shape as the swell of the same hips as before, the downward curve to the waist and a rising line of what would be ribs and the delicate curve of armpit leading to shoulder. Again the braid would figure prominently, coiling over the waist with the ribbon dangling and the braid itself loosened, suggesting a loss of composure and lack of restraint. This could easily be her favorite canvas — her favorite of what she would allow to be exhibited.

The fifth was hers and hers alone. Her heart was in every stroke. It would be all she ever had. Jackie's face, her eyes, her lips, slightly parted. "Jackie Saying Yes" was for Leah's comfort. The blue and gold of her eyes, the black lights in her hair, the sweet, pale pink of her lips.

The next day she worked in a bluish gray to outline the figures and a reddened gray to fill. She

173

found that she had properly gauged the amount of rubine underneath, and in the right places the skin color took on a richer tone. The flesh looked transparent, which should, she thought, tempt the viewer to concentrate and try to see through the paint to the real woman.

Day after day she continued with new shades, each layer building the figure and suggesting where the body was the warmest. She spent days on the backgrounds alone, painting white on white until she really thought she would touch cotton sheeting when the paint dried.

It took nearly a week for her to produce an acceptable braid with the pewter strips. She left the incoming messages on the answering machine and only when she was done, the braids anchored into the canvases and the canvases coated with the last sealers did she feel she could rest. Butch sat meaningfully by her empty dish when Leah went into the kitchen. The answering machine blinked frantically.

She treated them both to steak and added a half bottle of wine for herself. She replayed the messages and found that Valentina had called five times with lengthy pleas for Leah to call her back. A telemarketer wanted her to refinance her home. Constance's messages went from "I'm not really speaking to you, but you have to call me this minute" to "If you don't call me, I'll sue." Maureen had called once about a fundraiser and Jackie had not called at all. Well, Leah had promised she would call her. She wondered what Jackie was doing, who Jackie had met.

When her appetite was sated she treated Butch to

a long, thorough brushing followed by a walk to the riding school and along one of the trails. Butch was panting happily when they got back to the house and ran barking to the woman who clambered out of the T-bird at the sight of them.

"Didn't you get my messages? Do you have any idea what happens next Sunday?" Constance's agitation was such that she was standing on tiptoe. "The photographer from the *Chronicle* Sunday magazine is taking pictures for the magazine spread and you haven't even begun the installation!"

Leah froze and stared at Constance. "Oh my God. I completely forgot. I'm so sorry —"

"I've been trying to reach you for days! All you had to do was call. I don't care if you do have some new lover, this was really irresponsible of you —"

"I don't have a new lover. What gave you that —"

"I never let my feelings interfere with business, and it's really —"

"Will you stop for a minute," Leah demanded. "If we're going to yell at each other, we can at least do it in the house." She turned and led the way into the house, not waiting to see if Constance would follow. Her cheeks burned and she hoped none of her neighbors had been watching.

Constance's heels echoed in the hallway as she followed Leah to the kitchen. Leah offered Constance coffee and received a stony look in reply.

"I'm sorry, I should have called. I was working and without Sharla to keep me on a schedule I forgot about everything, including eating. You could have said why you were calling, you know." She wouldn't tell Constance she'd only just listened to the machine.

Constance stared at her shoes, two-toned leather

heels that made her calves look even longer and more shapely. Leah wondered why she couldn't accept the passing pleasure Constance had offered.

"I'm very sorry," she said again.

"Where is she?" Constance raised her head and stared unhappily across the kitchen at Leah.

"I have no idea. I'm not seeing her."

"I would have sworn she...well. I should have left a better message, I guess," Constance admitted. "I was going to drive over here a couple of days ago...I was jealous. And envious. I know I didn't offer you forever, but I wanted more than a day."

"I sorry I can't give you more."

There was a heavy silence, then Constance shook herself. "You were working? I hope you're going to tell me that the *Painted Moon* is done."

"They were done just a few days after you were here last. I've been working on something new for the last —" She glanced at the calendar — "good God, month. I'd like to add them to the show, but hung in a different area. They'll show everyone I really am back."

"I'll have to see them," Constance said. She smiled more like the Constance Leah knew best. "I'd love to see them."

Leah made a piffing sound and led the way to her workshop.

The canvases were arranged in a circle, gleaming from the still drying sealer. She stood aside and let Constance into their circle and waited for her reaction. They felt right to her, but Constance's opinion meant a lot.

Constance turned slowly. When she came to the last painting, the only one that was obviously Jackie, her fists clenched. She turned the full circle once more and then looked at Leah with a burning gaze.

"They are beautiful. Like nothing you've done before," she said huskily. Then, vehemently, she said, "But I won't exhibit any of them. I advise you with all my heart and experience, never to show any of them publicly. Ever."

Leah's jaw dropped. "What? What do you mean?"

Constance blinked and shook her head slightly. "You really don't know, do you? You don't see it."

"See what? They're nudes. I won't show that one," Leah said, pointing at the one that featured Jackie's face. "But the others are —"

"Lesbian. They're lesbian."

"You're going to have to explain that," Leah said. "Everyone knows I'm a lesbian."

"Yes, but you've never put it in your work before."

"Who and what I am is in everything I do." Leah's voice rose.

"It was never explicit before. These are nudes, these are paintings by a woman in love with another woman." Constance's voice rose to match Leah's.

"You make that sound dirty. I've never hidden it. I won't start now."

"I can't show them. I don't want my gallery labeled and I won't let you be labeled either."

"But everyone knows!" Leah was almost shouting now.

"Being labeled in the art world is degrading. You know that as well as I do! A 'woman' artist, a 'black' artist, a 'homeless' artist — all less than just plain Artist. That's the way it is. The way it has always been."

"I can't believe this is you talking. You've exhibited the most daring artists in the country."

"But never in a ghetto context. If I let you show even one of these you won't be Lee Beck, American Artist, but Lee Beck, Lesbian Artist. No matter what you do after that, 'lesbian' will always be in the description."

Leah jabbed her finger at Constance. "Do you have any idea how homophobic you sound?"

"I'm a realist. Art should transcend labels —"

"What about *illuminating* labels?"

"Do you want to be another Mapplethorpe?"

"I would be in fine company if I were. And there's nothing explicit in these paintings. If you see explicit lesbian content, that's your eyes putting it there."

Constance drew in an angry breath. "Everyone's eyes will put it there. As you said, everyone knows you're a lesbian. If you weren't, these might pass as explorations of the female form, but since you are, they're —"

"An exploration of the female form —"

"A glorification of female love." Constance stamped her foot. "You just don't get it. You're going to lose your standing as a leader in American arts."

"You're just afraid the *gallery* will lose its standing. You just don't want your walls sullied with lesbian work. Only your sheets."

Constance was trembling with anger. "I have

promoted dozens of gay men and lesbians in my gallery, like you."

"Don't wave your credentials at me! Obviously, you promoted the ones who were content to remain invisible." She gestured at the paintings. "I think this is the best work I've ever done. Are you telling me you won't exhibit it?"

Constance took a deep breath, obviously fighting for control. "Can't we argue about this after the opening of *Painted Moon?*"

"No," Leah said stubbornly. "I want this series exhibited. It's called *Yes*. It's important to me."

Constance bit her lower lip and clenched and unclenched her fists. "Why are you making me do this?"

"Maybe it's time for us both to renounce being invisible. To not run from the label, but to use it and not let anyone make it an insult."

"You can be so incredibly naive."

Leah stared at Constance's unyielding expression. Until now, she had trusted Constance's judgment without question. Abruptly her anger dissolved. She looked at the paintings again and realized how Constance saw them. How most people would see them.

Sensuous, even erotic. Not exploring the female form, but worshipping it. Painted by a woman in love, in lust, in the heat of passion for another woman. Desire and longing mingled with intimate understanding of the texture and heat of the female body. Would anyone but another woman know that the small of a woman's back is slightly darker, slightly hotter than her shoulders? That her hips are cooler, her thighs smoother?

Leah sighed and felt exhausted. "You're right. I wouldn't have been prepared for the fallout." Starting over on her reputation was untenable — she couldn't be a beginner again.

"You're finally talking sense."

"Let me think about it," Leah said slowly. "I need to think it through."

"You *will* install *Painted Moon* before the photographer gets there, right?"

Leah nodded.

Constance left the circle of the paintings and stood next to Leah. "I'm sorry I got upset. Maybe that's a tribute to your work. They would stir people up. I didn't know — I didn't know I felt that strongly."

"I don't know how I feel." She looked forlornly at the paintings. "I thought I'd already come out."

Constance patted Leah's cheek. "Why don't I meet you at the gallery tomorrow at one?"

Leah nodded. "Can you see yourself out?"

"Sure."

She listened to the sound of the T-bird's engine, then sat down on the floor and looked at her work. The daylight faded and she got stiffly to her feet. She covered the canvases and went to the dark house wishing that Sharla were there to tell her what to do. She longed to call Jackie, but what was left of her courage failed her completely.

"You've sunk to a new low," Jackie told herself. "You should have made a date. It's just because you've got nothing to do on a Saturday night that you want to call her." There had been a month of Saturday nights with nothing to do. When she didn't make an effort to go out and keep herself diverted, she sat around and thought about Leah. She had grown to loathe her apartment's tiny kitchen and dark light. Thank God for her job — the work was absorbing and rewarding. But at night she brooded.

If she didn't do something tonight, she'd lose her self-respect. She remembered how she had accused Leah of being obsessed with Sharla, but now she understood a little more about obsession and love. Leah had rejected her, but it didn't make her stop hoping. She had to try one more time.

Examine your motives, she told herself. Your mother arrives at the end of next week and could it be you want to be able to introduce her to Leah the artist and Leah your lover? Pipe dreams. Why couldn't she be content to show her mother the first set of drawings she'd done on her own for a client assigned to her? Drawings Angela herself had admired.

Do it or shut up, she told herself.

Her finger trembled on the buttons. She took two rapid, deep breaths and listened to the ring. The phone was answered with a click and the familiar sound of a taped greeting.

She gathered her composure and waited for the beep. "Hi, Leah, this is Jackie. Um, Jackie Frakes. I hope you remem — of course you do. I was just calling, um . . ." She berated herself for sounding like an idiot. "I was calling because . . ."

The receiver was suddenly lifted. "I'm here."

Jackie swallowed and couldn't find her voice.

"Are you there?"

"Yes. I, well, I've been thinking and I . . . the way we parted. I think we need to talk about it. At least I need to."

There was a long silence. Then Leah said, "I think so too. Would you like to come to my place?"

"I'd love to," Jackie said. "Are you busy now . . . I'm so, there's no particular urgency except I . . . well. I'd like to clear things up."

"Tonight would be great." Leah told her how to find the house and Jackie hung up after offering to bring something for dinner and scribbling down Leah's directions to a Thai take-out not far from her home.

She changed into something comfortable and realized as she walked to her car that she had chosen clothes that flattered her figure and came off easily. She sat for a moment in the car and came to a decision. She would seduce Leah if she could. She would take her to bed and do everything she could to make Leah want her to stay there. She knew she was competing with Sharla's memory. If she had even the remotest chance of meaning something to Leah, then she wanted to seize it. She could handle being second best in Leah Beck's eyes.

She hoped she looked more self-confident than she felt. Some of her tension eased as she listened to Butch barking hysterically and Leah's scolding as

Leah opened the door. Leah took the bag of take out and Butch danced around Jackie. Jackie found herself on the floor fending off Butch's slobbery, happy hellos. She could wish Leah would show her this much affection, she thought.

Butch finally let her up and followed Jackie to the kitchen.

Leah smiled and pointed at the sink. "There's soap."

Jackie laughed and washed her face. "I guess Butch missed me," she said as she dried herself.

"Butch isn't the only one," Leah said quietly.

Jackie's heart leapt as she met Leah's gaze. She trembled, aware that her passion hadn't dimmed. She didn't feel as helpless as she had at the art gallery, as reliant on Leah's direction. But she wanted Leah in the same deep, needful way. In a way that excluded wanting Ina or any other woman. "That's good to know," she said and tried to let her eyes talk for her.

Leah look away and fetched plates and cutlery. They shared pad thai noodles and chicken satay over jasmine rice at the counter in Leah's spacious kitchen. They ate quickly and talked little. Jackie would have asked for a tour of the house to see if it matched the Shaker style of the kitchen, but she wanted to move onto more important things. She could see the house anytime. And she had every intention of seeing the bedroom before the night was out.

Leah had already made coffee and they went into the backyard to enjoy the mild evening.

Jackie loved the garden, though it needed some attention. A high fence and two beautiful oaks gave it an enclosed feeling. Jackie realized the garden gave way to a steep slope. A retaining wall would slow down erosion if sink posts could be stabilized. A building too oddly shaped for a garage stood to one side. "What's that?"

"My workshop," Leah said, waving a hand at the small detached building. Jackie followed Leah through the garden to the small gazebo.

"Are you working on anything?"

"I just finished. I don't know when — if — it'll be exhibited." She didn't elaborate. "I spent this afternoon hauling the *Painted Moon* series to a gallery in San Francisco. It goes on exhibit this Friday night. I have to finish the installation before tomorrow at two. For a photographer." She sat down on the bench and Jackie hesitated a moment, then straddled the bench so she could look at Leah.

"That was fast," Jackie said.

"It was an unexpected opening. You met the owner, Constance . . . the woman at the gallery when we were leaving."

"Oh," Jackie said. She hoped the darkness hid her blush. "I wasn't exactly at my best."

"I wouldn't say that," Leah said, almost reluctantly, with a hint of teasing in her voice.

Jackie's face burned. "Leah, I . . ."

"It's okay," Leah said quickly. "You don't have to say anything."

"Okay, I won't," Jackie said. She set her coffee cup down on the railing. Leah looked at her in surprise as she took Leah's cup out of her hand and set it on the railing as well.

Jackie took a deep breath and tried to find her courage. Her voice was a whisper. "Let me show you, then."

A light breeze shifted the oaks and the moonlight flickered across Leah's face. Jackie trembled, aware that she had never done anything like this before, but knowing that the content and form of her entire future rested on her ability to convey how she felt. She had to make Leah understand.

She slowly lifted the hem of her sweater and pulled it up over her head. Her bra unhooked in the front and she unsnapped it, exposing herself in the moonlight.

"Jackie . . ." Leah swallowed convulsively. "You don't —"

Jackie put her fingers across Leah's lips. "I do." She slid off the bench to her knees. She stared up at Leah and said intensely, "Let me show you."

Leah's legs opened and Jackie slipped between them, pressing her naked breasts to Leah's waist. This time she mastered the buttons of Leah's shirt without fumbling and her tongue moistened a path across the plain of Leah's chest and flicked at each hardening tip.

She felt Leah's hands come to her breasts and caress the soft sides. Encouraged, she continued her slow adoration of Leah's body, exploring her ribs and stomach with her tongue and kissing her way to the waist of Leah's jeans. She felt at peace with herself and in tune with Leah's body.

She could sense the gradual increase in Leah's skin temperature and simultaneously feel the prickle of gooseflesh along Leah's back as the cool night air whispered across it. She could hear the tiniest changes in Leah's breathing, sounds that could have been the beginnings of moans. In the moonlight she could see the light and dark of Leah's breasts and her mouth sought the dark tips with more pressure in response to the quiver that rippled through Leah's body.

She pressed her palm to the seam of Leah's jeans and felt Leah's hips rise in response, meeting the warmth of her hand. She smiled to herself, content to know that if nothing else, she aroused Leah. She drew Leah's head down for a lingering kiss, finishing with the brush of her tongue on the corner of Leah's mouth. Leah's hips surged against Jackie's palm.

Jackie stood up and offered her bare breasts to Leah's mouth. On impulse, Jackie undid the band at the bottom of her braid and worked her fingers through it while Leah's mouth made love to her breasts. She let her hair fall around Leah's head and shoulders.

Leah groaned and raised her head, then pulled Jackie onto her lap, burying her face in Jackie's abundance of hair. Leah kissed it and with hungry urgency returned to Jackie's breasts.

Jackie reluctantly stood up. "Show me your bed," she said softly.

Leah looked up at her as if Jackie had asked to be shown to the moon. Leah's gaze fell to Jackie's breasts again, and she leaned forward to kiss them again.

"Let's go to bed, Leah," Jackie said, moving away. She took Leah's hands and drew her to her feet.

Leah swayed and didn't move at first, then she led Jackie back through the garden and into the house. She tore the covers back from the bed and feverishly shoved the soft leggings Jackie wore down until Jackie could kick them completely off. She pushed Jackie down on the bed and knelt, her mouth returning to Jackie's breasts.

Jackie shuddered with pleasure, thrilling to the rough texture of Leah's jeans against her thighs. Leah abandoned Jackie's breasts and knelt between Jackie's legs, sank her mouth into Jackie with a deep groan.

Jackie twisted her hips up and she felt a frighteningly powerful contraction which gave way to the first trembling waves of climax. She hadn't meant to ... she clutched Leah's head, held it to her and didn't fight the rising tide. She let her pleas tumble out of her throat and rode the crest of her passion, simultaneously wishing to stay in this moment of ecstasy forever and pushing it aside to pull Leah into her arms, kissing her deeply, tasting herself in Leah's mouth, on Leah's face. She unbuttoned and unzipped Leah's jeans and slid her hand inward and down-ward.

Her body was vibrating like a plucked string. Through her quivering fingertips she felt Leah's throbbing wetness and rewarded her with the teasing strokes she liked. Surely Leah could tell that Jackie loved her, loved doing this to her.

Leah responded by lifting her hips, giving Jackie room. "Please. Jackie, please."

She could feel each grip of Leah's muscles. Leah sighed with pleasure and Jackie intended to go as slowly as possible. She tried to remain true to her intentions, but her mouth thirsted for Leah and, unable to help herself, she let her tongue seek out the delicious flesh. Leah groaned and pulled Jackie's hair up over her stomach.

Jackie was aware only of the sensations her tongue and fingers sent her. The sensuality of Leah's body surrounding her fingers, so wet, so yielding but so strong. The heady taste of Leah on her tongue, filling her mouth. She devoted herself to revelling in the beauty of Leah's response and the explosion of her passion.

Like an old radio coming on, sounds gradually reached Jackie's ears over the thud of her own rapid heartbeat. Leah's ragged breathing penetrated first, then another sound, a stifled sob.

She gathered Leah in her arms and let her cry, wondering if she should be gratified or concerned. She stroked Leah's hair and shushed her and waited.

Leah fumbled next to the bed and came up with a Kleenex. She blew her nose and mumbled, "Sorry."

"It's okay." Jackie tried for humor. She scratched her crotch and said in as gravelly a tone as she could manage, "All my women cry."

Leah laughed a little. "I'll bet they do."

All laughter gone, Jackie said, "There's only you, you know."

Leah's smile faded but she didn't say anything. She pulled Jackie into her arms and they snuggled down into the bed.

Now's the time to tell her, Jackie thought. Say *I love you*. The words formed, but Leah stirred slightly and pulled the covers over them.

"Go to sleep," Leah whispered.

To her surprise, Jackie did.

14

Leah stirred at the sound of a voice and a woof from Butch.

"You know you don't like orange juice, you know you don't."

Jackie's voice. Leah smiled, remembering the cabin. Birds were making a racket outside and white sunshine peeked through the curtains. It looked like a lovely day.

She went to the bathroom and then headed for the kitchen wrapped in her robe. She watched Jackie for a moment, the sunlight draped on her shoulders, her hair like spun obsidian. She was wearing Leah's National Center for Lesbian Rights T-shirt and nothing else.

Jackie smiled at her. "You're blushing."

"No I'm not," Leah said weakly. "I'm just warm."

Jackie laughed and, to Leah's relief, let it go. "You know you don't have any food in here, don't you? Butch is pretty upset about the food situation in general."

Ignorant of Leah's glare, Butch thumped her tail emphatically on the floor.

"I'm starving," Jackie said, her head deep in the refrigerator. "Ah! Well, it's something." She emerged with a package of pre-peeled carrots.

They munched happily in silence, sharing the orange juice between them, until Leah realized they were smiling at each other like idiots.

"About last night," Leah said, then she stopped.

"What about it?"

Leah felt her blush return. "I don't know what to say."

Jackie pursed her lips with a smirk. "Well, I do. Fantastic for starters."

"Well, yes, that does about cover it." She stared at her carrot.

"Lee, look at me."

Leah looked. Saw the sable hair, the translucent skin. She tried to see to the woman underneath.

"Let's go back to bed," Jackie said softly. "I'd really like to."

"I should feed Butch," Leah said.

"Well, then feed her," Jackie said with a laugh.

Leah bustled around the kitchen knowing that

two pairs of eyes watched, both with hunger. Butch devoted her attention to her dish when it hit the floor, but Leah could feel Jackie's gaze on her. Leah washed her hands, wiped out the sink, dried her hands, mopped the counter and finally stood twisting the dish towel into a knot. She knew what she wanted. She wanted it so much she couldn't put it into words.

Jackie's lips grazed the back of her neck. Her body's response was immediate and alarming. She broke out into a cold sweat and her knees trembled. Jackie's hands clasped her hips gently and the tip of her tongue feathered under one ear. Leah gasped and Jackie pulled the robe open and gently stroked Leah's breasts.

"You want to, don't you?" Jackie's voice held a plea, though Leah thought the answer was obvious from the hard ache of her breasts. "Say yes." Jackie's voice broke. "Please say yes."

In answer Leah turned to kiss Jackie. Her eyes closed and she felt as though she were slipping down a long water slide into a volcano.

Jackie's hands finally left Leah alone long enough for Leah to catch her breath. Exhausted, she stretched out on the bed. "For a beginner," she murmured, "you certainly know your stuff."

Jackie's answer was a satisfied smile.

"How do you know?"

Jackie's eyebrows arched and she turned her head. "Know what?"

"What I want. When I don't know myself."

Jackie's expression was now definitely smug. "Your body talks to me." The Cheshire grin returned.

Leah tried to recall why she had wanted to give Jackie freedom. None of the reasons made any sense. She didn't want Jackie to find someone else. She wanted to be side by side with Jackie.

Leah looked at her. Love, she thought. I'm in love. With *this* woman, and if she doesn't want to be with me, I won't get another chance. She didn't know what to do or say. She felt a little giddy. She didn't want to scare Jackie away.

"I have to be in the city by two," Leah said. "The photographer."

Jackie said, "Then we have a little more time." Without opening her eyes she trailed her fingertips over Leah's ribs.

"Oh no you don't," Leah said, pushing the hand away. "I couldn't possibly, not one more time."

Jackie smirked. "That's what you said last time."

"This time I'm sure," Leah said. "And I'm starving. Let's go have some lunch."

Jackie rolled onto her side and rested on one elbow. A Venus, Leah thought. A Venus I'd walk a Milo for. She was definitely giddy.

Jackie quirked an eyebrow. "What's so funny?"

Leah shook her head. "We can shower together if you promise no tricks." She had to get some distance back. Her head was spinning and she didn't trust her instincts.

Jackie promised with mock sincerity while she plainly crossed her fingers, but within a half-hour they were both dressed and out the front door. Jackie followed Leah to a diner in San Leandro that specialized in English breakfasts. They ate indulgently and talked about everything except when they would see each other next.

♥ ♥ ♥ ♥ ♥

Why doesn't she ask me to come with her to the gallery, Jackie wondered. Why doesn't she say when she wants to see me?

The bill came and Leah scooped it up. "You bought dinner, remember? Be right back."

Jackie watched Leah walk to the register. She seemed so composed. Jackie didn't know if she had successfully made a dent in Leah's life. Would Leah miss her this evening? Maybe Leah just didn't understand that Jackie wanted to go on together. What more could she have done?

Said *I love you.* The ultimate risk. Just say it, she told herself. But she couldn't, not when she knew the answer. Sharla. Why ask for, why even expect something she couldn't have?

She had told herself she'd be happy as second best. She wondered how often she told herself lies.

Leah returned and put down the tip. "Ready?"

Jackie followed her to the parking lot, then leaned against the truck. "When will the magazine be out?"

"Next weekend, to coincide with the opening. The story's already done, apparently. Printing presses are waiting even as we speak."

"Well, I won't keep you," Jackie said. She

swallowed the lump in her throat — her pride, probably — and said, "When can I see you again?"

After a long moment, Leah said, "When would you like to?"

Tonight, Jackie thought. Tomorrow morning. Every night. She said, trying for a light approach, "I don't know how lesbians do this."

"You're free to do whatever you want," Leah said. Her lashes were low, hiding her expression.

Jackie sighed. Leah clearly didn't want to make any plans, clearly didn't want Jackie in her future. With a flash of anger she said, "That's good. I need lots of room. So many women, so little time."

Leah nodded. "I know what you mean."

Jackie finally blinked and said, "Well, you have a photographer waiting. I'm looking forward to seeing the exhibit."

"Perhaps I'll see you there, then."

Jackie didn't trust herself to speak. She made a show of driving swiftly away, as though she too had somewhere important to be. She spent the rest of the day slamming cupboard doors and asking herself what she had for brains.

Leah watched Jackie drive away and said to the rear view mirror, "Well, that didn't go how I thought it would." Now, of course, there was nothing wrong with her vocal cords. They hadn't been operating a few minutes earlier. Neither had her brain.

That moment next to the truck had been like standing on the edge of a precipice knowing that all the best of life was at the bottom. All she had to do was be willing to free-fall. Why hadn't she just said she'd drop by Jackie's place after the photographer finished? Why hadn't she told Jackie she was in love with her?

Telling Sharla she loved her had been easy — words had never been a problem. Their friendship had paved the way to easier communication when they became lovers. With Jackie she had precious opportunities that she kept screwing up. Words she felt inadequate to say because she wasn't sure Jackie wanted to hear or believe them.

She drove home as quickly as possible and dashed into her workshop. She carefully loaded the four *Yes* canvases into the truck.

Once she was on the freeway she second-guessed herself. She didn't want to start over on her reputation as an artist. But the work was the best she had ever done. She didn't relish controversy. But the highest art pushed at people's minds.

She hadn't wanted to display the paintings before Jackie saw them. At the same time she felt the only way to show Jackie how she felt was to tell the world. How would Jackie respond, she wondered. That Jackie liked having sex with her — that was monumentally clear. What if Jackie wanted nothing more?

Everything was still a muddle. Mushy, incoherent gray.

* * *

She got to the gallery early and Constance wasn't there yet. As she set down the last canvas she heard Constance's rapid footsteps behind her. Leah turned to look at her, feeling as frightened and defiant as a teenager caught after curfew.

"You're out of your mind," Constance said.

"Yes, I think you're right. But I have to."

"Why? Why now?" Constance came closer, lowering her voice.

"Because . . . I am starting over. Because who I am now isn't who I was, even when I did *Painted Moon*. Overnight I changed. Because I fell in love again."

"Darling, I don't understand."

"I think . . . what you said was right. About not putting any lesbian content in my work before. I was out, but I wasn't *out*." She bit her lower lip. "I'm in love. I don't think she loves me back, but I can't think of any other way to prove it to her. And I need to prove it to myself. I'm afraid . . . I'm afraid if I hide this work I'll forget that I could love someone again. And I'll go back to the mountains and hide . . ." She choked and Constance put an arm around her.

"You're out of your mind, but I love you for it."

"I can't go on hiding, I want to be out in the light again. Where Jackie can see me. Where Sharla would want me to be. So —"

"You're taking the bull by the horns and screaming for the world to take a long, hard look at you. All of you. In my gallery." She squeezed Leah briskly and let her go. "Hell."

Jackie paused in the doorway and caught her mother's eye. She gave a tiny wave and Jellica winked at her. A man with a warbly voice and smoker's cough didn't seem to be running out of breath any time soon, and Jackie thought she'd rescue her mother in a few minutes if she hadn't already extricated herself. Jellica would be tired, having arrived just this afternoon and been transported directly to the museum.

Jackie used the spare minutes to examine her mother's work again. The last time she had seen it was in London when she'd joined her parents at its unveiling. She stood at the back of the room and watched the crowd mill around the sculpture. They rubbed their hands as though they were stepping up to a fire. *Weavers* was indeed warm, inviting, comforting. The three figures could have been anyone's grandmothers. From their fingertips, yarns streamed in all colors. How, Jackie wondered, had her mother so accurately gauged the drape of yarn when carving it.

The warbly man was still talking, so Jackie crossed the room and said in a worried tone, "Won't we be late?"

The warbly man said, "Oh, are you going to the Reardon opening? I never miss it."

"I don't think so," Jellica said.

"It's one of the leading art galleries in the country. A new exhibit tonight. I'm sure there will be no problem with your getting in."

"Maybe we will," Jackie said, "but we're running late for a dinner engagement."

The warbly man finally went away and her

197

mother gave Jackie a prolonged hug. "So good to see you. There, that hug's from your father. He demands a full report from me on the state of your happiness. That turquoise is pretty on you." She pushed Jackie away and studied her face. "My demand at the moment is dinner. Where?"

Jackie laughed. "Nob Hill. It's quiet and we can talk all we want."

"Starting with your love life. You have a new set of worry lines."

Jackie wrinkled her nose. "It's really not fair that you can read my mind."

"Mother's privilege."

They linked arms and left the gallery, stopped only a half-dozen times by curators, art students, the fundraiser and an aide to the mayor. The last pressed tickets to the Reardon opening on them, saying he wanted an international *artiste* like Jellica Frakes to know that San Francisco was a hotbed of artistic discovery.

"It seems the whole world is going there," Jellica said as they got in the cab.

Jackie turned the tickets over and read the full name of the gallery. No, she thought. The world's not this small. But Leah had said she was opening her exhibit tonight. At "Constance's" gallery. And the big opening was at the Constance Reardon Gallery. "Maybe we should go," Jackie said. "But first I'll fill you in on my love life. It's sort of relevant."

Mason's was elegant and quiet, and served, on Angela's recommendation, a killer chocolate souffle.

Through appetizers and the house's specialty filet mignon, Jackie related the entire story. Toward the end of it she found it hard to tell. Her reasons for alternatively staying away from and then seducing Leah started to sound flimsy. Her evidence of Leah's continuing devotion to Sharla seemed a little thin.

"It sounds to me like you're running away from the truth."

"I'm not running from anything." Jackie studied the point of her fork.

"You *do* think you deserve love, don't you?"

"Of course I do . . . why wouldn't I?"

"I've been doing some reading." Her mother sipped her water and didn't meet Jackie's gaze. "Researchers suggest that some . . . homosexuals subconsciously sabotage their relationships. They feel they don't deserve happiness because they live in sin."

"That's absurd," Jackie said. "I don't . . . that's ridiculous."

"I had to ask. You aren't behaving in a completely rational way."

"But, Mom," Jackie said, "I know I'm right about what Leah wants. She's said exactly nothing. And I tried to give her the chance to say she wanted to see me again." She put down her fork and stared dolefully across the table. "And, well, I can't tell her how I feel because there's no point. She'd just feel guilty. She'd stop seeing me for my own good. Not that she's seeing me now, but you know what I mean."

Her mother rolled her eyes and ate the last bite of her filet mignon. "If you say so, dear. But eventually you're going to tell her. I know that much about you."

"Maybe so. But by then, maybe she'll love me just a little. Maybe want me around." She hung her head. No, she thought, I can't live that way. I can't start the family I want on those terms.

"*Petit cherie,*" her mother said, her tone admonishing.

Jackie nodded and folded her napkin. "I take it all back. I can't live on scraps." She sighed and stared at the ceiling for a moment, then looked back at her mother. She managed a wry smile. "Be sure to tell Dad that I'm in love and boy am I happy."

The waitress returned to collect their plates and asked if they'd like dessert.

"My daughter and I both require a chocolate souffle. Extra sauce."

Jackie laughed. "Chocolate cures everything, doesn't it?"

"And gives the extra edge you'll need to walk into that gallery. To say hello and it looks nice and pretend you're not in love — that will take a great deal of chocolate." Her mother tilted her head with a philosophical air. "*Bon appetit.*"

♥ ♥ ♥ ♥ ♥

"Someone take an axe and split me down the middle," Leah muttered at Constance, who shot her an I-told-you-so look as Leah kept going. She had spent most of the night walking back and forth between the two rooms. She'd just finish talking to one critic about *Painted Moon* when VIPs demanded a word with her about *Yes*. To Constance's delight, three of the *Painted Moon* canvases were sold already, and one of the *Yes* series.

In response to the critic from the *Los Angeles Times*, she said that no, she didn't believe *Yes* was indicative of her future work. Nor was *Painted Moon.* She said the same thing to a reporter from *The Advocate.* One look at her history would show that she rarely used a previous series as a foundation for the next.

Maureen and Valentina had been wonderful, kissing and hugging her and adding simple, heartfelt praise. They'd melted into the crowd when Associated Press asked her opinion, as a lesbian artist, about censorship.

The questions seemed endless. Yes, she was pleased with both series. Yes, she was a lesbian. Yes, she had used a live model. No, she would not give the model's name. No, she did not consider herself a gay activist. Yes, she believed in gay civil rights. Yes, she considered herself a feminist. Yes, she supposed that if *Painted Moon* celebrated winter — which she wasn't really sure it did — then *Yes* celebrated women.

She wanted to say many times, "What a stupid question." And "Why have you never asked me about my sexuality before?" And "When are you going to ask me about the work, not my lesbianism?"

Constance had been right. Dead right.

"Darling, Jellica Frakes just came in." Constance's whisper was loaded with excitement. "She's looking at

Moon Pines. I can tell she likes it, likes it very much."

Leah felt as though Constance had dashed her with icy water. "Is she alone?"

Constance frowned. "Jackie's with her."

"Does she like it, can you tell?"

"Go see for yourself," Constance said. "Hell, woman, show some spine."

Leah peeked through the doorway separating *Painted Moon* from *Yes.* Jackie's face was animated with eagerness and flushed with a delicate pink as she pointed at the canvases. A woman with salt-and-pepper hair stood next to her and listened. That must be Jellica, Leah thought.

An art critic descended on them, but after a minute Jellica linked her arm with Jackie's and moved to the last canvas. Leah didn't think her heart could beat any faster. They would be coming in to see *Yes* any minute.

♥ ♥ ♥ ♥ ♥

"It all comes back to me so vividly," Jackie said. "You would have loved the powder. And the quiet."

The man standing next to them cleared his throat. "Would you say this is a metaphor for winter?"

Jackie frowned at him. He was tiresome and his grunge-beatnik attire looked pretentious on someone pushing fifty.

Her mother said drily, "It can hardly be a metaphor for the obvious subject matter."

Jackie, her eyes opened innocently wide, said,

"Perhaps it is a metaphor for weather." She felt her mother tremble with a smothered laugh.

"Ah, yes, I see what you mean," the man said. "I would be most interested to know your reaction to the other series."

Jackie stared at him blankly.

"In the next room. It is remarkably different. Almost hard to believe it's the same artist. Looking at this series one would never suspect ... well, as I said, I would be interested in your reaction."

Jackie surreptitiously glanced around for any sign of Leah as she followed her mother into the second room. The canvases here were arranged so they had to be viewed individually.

Jellica came to a sudden stop in front of the first one. Jackie closed her eyes for a moment, then studied the painting again. As her mother was saying, it was striking. The bend of the knee into the swell of thigh, the curving line of hip. It was sensuous. She puzzled for a moment as to why, then it came to her. It was the angle — until recently Jackie wouldn't have recognized it. The painting captured what you would see if you were looking down a woman's body with your cheek a few inches above her stomach. She had seen Leah from that angle. Her fingers had been teasing Leah. Leah's hips had been moving —

Her cheeks grew warm with the memory. Her heart thudded against her ribs. Leah had captured a moment of complete intimacy without any explicit body parts and yet the woman in the painting seethed with sex. She was undoubtedly created out of passion.

Looking at the painting, Jackie understood better

why Leah still felt longing for Sharla. Until now she had been a vague figure in Jackie's mind.

"I can hardly wait to see more," her mother said.

Her heart slowly breaking, Jackie dreaded the next picture.

At the third canvas, Jackie gasped, staggering back from it, stunned at the sight of a braid woven into the canvas. Her mother looked at the painting, then at Jackie's hair, then back at the painting.

Jackie hovered between emotional states, so flabbergasted she didn't know where to land. This luxurious sweep of shoulder and ribs and delicate point of elbow — that couldn't be how Leah saw her! She wasn't — she didn't look like that. So —

The man who had been dogging their heels said, "You wouldn't be the model, would you?"

Leah heard the question and groaned to herself. She should have realized! Everyone would take one look at Jackie's braid and know she was the model. Jackie's face was stained with red and Jellica looked — murderous. She wilted into Constance. "I'm getting out of here."

"You can't," Constance hissed.

"If I stay there'll be a scene and you don't want that." Without waiting for Connie's answer, Leah slunk from the room. She had thought she would show Jackie how much she loved her. Instead, she'd given Jackie ample reason to hate her.

♥ ♥ ♥ ♥ ♥

Jackie swallowed noisily and decided to ignore the question. She pushed ahead to the last canvas. People were making room for her. They were staring. They all knew it was her. They all knew — or suspected with good reason — that she had had an affair with Leah Beck.

They all knew she was a lesbian. In a flash she remembered Sharla's gravestone, the word *sinner* and she felt naked. She studied the last canvas — her braid coming undone, her breast, her shoulder.

She clenched her fists and her embarrassment exploded into fiery anger. She would find Leah Beck and — and there wouldn't be anything left when she was done.

Jackie spun on her heel and marched out of the room.

"*Petit cherie*," her mother called. Jackie stopped and let her mother catch up to her. "What does it mean?"

"I don't know," Jackie said. "I can't — I need some time." She was so angry she thought she would burst into tears.

"I can find my way back to the hotel," her mother said, with a sympathetically angry light in her eye. "Call me tomorrow morning?"

Jackie nodded. She escaped into the night and walked numbly down to Market Street. That it was eight blocks hardly penetrated. She automatically descended into the Muni station and waited twenty long minutes for her streetcar. The three blocks from her stop to the apartment were a blur and when she finally sat down in her darkened apartment, she couldn't remember climbing the stairs.

15

Leah opened the door with trepidation. If she were to do a portrait of Jellica Frakes at that moment, she would simply sketch a glacier. A steel glacier.

"How did you find me?" Leah realized after she spoke that the question had a furtive ring to it. As though Jellica had a right to be hunting her down.

"The gallery owner didn't really want to give me your address but I insisted. The cab driver had a map."

Leah couldn't blame Constance. She had the

feeling that few people held out when Jellica Frakes insisted on something.

"Having come this far, I'd like to come in," Jellica said.

Leah stood aside and told Butch to go outside. Butch, after an unusually docile sniff at the visitor, complied.

Leah had hardly had time to steady her own nerves and come to grips with what she had done to Jackie by exhibiting *Yes*. She put her hands in the pockets of her blazer and faced Jellica across the living room.

After a long, steady look, Jellica said, "I thought I would try to talk to you as a peer and a fellow artist. But — well, artistic ethics pales as an issue right now. You have hurt my daughter. She didn't deserve that."

"I know," Leah mumbled miserably. "I didn't mean to hurt her. It was the last thing I wanted to do."

Jellica continued as though Leah hadn't spoken. "How dare you *play* with Jackie like that? Do you enjoy torture? Are you proud of the public humiliation she suffered?"

Jellica's voice rose and Leah withered under the force of it. She wanted to crawl back to the cabin and rot there. "I'm sorry. I'm so sorry. I wanted to show her how I felt."

"You showed her. You showed the world. I wish I could say the paintings were terrible, but they're pure genius. If it weren't Jackie I would have been the loudest with praise." Jellica's voice trembled. "You could have at least warned her. Did she mean so little to you? It's not that I am shocked or troubled by her being sexual. But now the whole world knows how and with whom and she had no preparation. *Mon dieu!* How can you paint like that and be so insensitive?"

Leah pressed a hand to her mouth and dropped into the nearest chair. "You didn't get it then? Dear God. She didn't either." Her eyes brimmed over, but she ignored the tears.

"Speaking purely as her mother, I warn you. Grovel, beg, do whatever it takes to help her recover from you or I will find every way possible to make your life hell."

Leah believed it. But she felt a spark of resentment. "I've said I was sorry. I'm — stunned about the way things turned out. I meant it to be different, but... some genius. I wanted to convey something very simple and she didn't get it. Neither did you."

Leah blinked away the tears and met Jellica's deep hazel gaze with a proud lift to her chin. "I love Jackie. I'm in love with her. I couldn't find the words — I didn't think she'd believe me unless I showed her somehow."

Jellica stared for a moment, then shook her head slightly. "With love must come respect and trust. Why didn't you respect her enough to show her the series before anyone else saw it, and trust that she would have understood. You can paint what you like, but you have a strange way of showing your love."

"Yes, I realize that now. Not that that gets me off the hook." Leah let her gaze drop. "I don't understand. She was all I thought about while I was working on them. Every color, brush stroke, every canvas..." A stray thought nagged at her and she groaned. "I'm a fool! I held back one of the canvases because I wanted to keep her anonymous." She laughed bitterly. "That failed completely. Everything failed." She hurried out the back door and into her workshop. She lifted the dust cover from *Jackie Saying Yes* and studied it.

Jellica was so right. The other four canvases were just the body. This canvas had Jackie's face, her eyes. This canvas completed the person and the five canvases together completed the message.

She carried it back to the house. She set the canvas down and turned to Jellica."I hope when you see this you'll understand —"

♥ ♥ ♥ ♥ ♥

Jackie stood next to her mother and her expression said she did not nor did she want to understand anything.

"You should have told me. Warned me. Showed them to me." Jackie folded her arms across her chest. "I felt like a fool. I felt like everyone was laughing at me because *they* knew you were conducting research in bed while I thought there was more to it." She looked acutely embarrassed by her mother's presence.

Jellica had stepped forward and was gazing at the canvas Leah had leaned against a chair. Leah heard Jellica's breath catch, but Jackie didn't glance up.

"Jackie, I'm so sorry," Leah said softly. "I just wanted — I'm trying — damn!" She covered her eyes with her hands. "Like a two-year old. I can't talk!"

Jellica said, "I think I'll find myself a glass of water."

"I don't know why I'm finding this so hard."

Leah cleared her throat. "It wasn't this way with Sharla."

"Do you do that deliberately?"

"Do what?"

"Sharla. Talk about her." Jackie's eyes were a snapping black. Leah could sense her fury.

"I can't help it. She was a big part of my life."

"I know that." Jackie squeezed her eyes shut for a moment, then opened them again, revealing a glimmer of tears. "Don't you think I know that? She doesn't have to be less. I just wanted a place of my own."

"You have . . . a place," Leah said.

Jackie flicked a glance at the canvas. "Not there."

"What about here?" Leah put her hand on her heart. "I never meant to hurt you. I should have warned you. I didn't know how to tell you. I didn't think you'd believe that I'd had enough time to fall in love with you. I wanted to show you. I —" Leah ran out of words. She knew she wasn't making sense. Helplessly, she waved a hand at the canvas.

Jackie didn't look at the painting. She stepped closer and said with the barest hint of a smile, "Do you believe you deserve happiness?"

"No," Leah said. "I don't deserve it. I don't deserve you." She spread her hands. "I had the love of my life. I still love her. It doesn't go away just because she's not here."

Jackie's voice was soft. "Can I fit in somewhere?"

"Everywhere." Leah smiled softly. "She left a lot of empty places. I made some more. And you fill them all up."

Jackie's lower lip trembled, then her chin lifted.

"I thought — I thought I could be second best. But I can't."

"You aren't. You're first. But I have to be honest. She will always be with me."

"I know. You can talk about her. You don't have to choose between your past and our future. In the here and now I —"

"I love you."

"— love you."

They shared a smile and then wrapped each other in welcoming arms.

"I've seen enough of the kitchen," a voice said. "Can I assume everything has been resolved satisfactorily?"

Jackie stepped away from Leah and cleared her throat. "We've come to an understanding."

"Good. I want to go to the hotel. It's been a very long day and I was supposed to call Eliza the *moment* I arrived."

Jackie fished in her pocket and came up with her keys. "The car's all yours."

Jellica turned to Leah with a wry grin. "How do you do. I've looked forward to meeting you for years. Somehow we skipped right over that part, didn't we?" She laughed and Leah recognized the joy of life Jellica had passed onto Jackie.

"I have been following your work for years," Leah said as soberly as she could manage. "It's an honor to meet you at last."

"Would you like to come to dinner tomorrow night? To celebrate your . . . oh dear. Would this be considered an . . . engagement?"

"Mom . . ."

"Yes," Leah said. "We were very bad at going steady, so I think we should just go to the next level and try harder."

"Good. We can talk about china patterns."

"Mom!"

Jellica laughed. "I'm teasing." She held out a hand to Leah, who grasped it firmly. "We can talk about your new career as a lesbian artist. You're going to get pigeonholed, you know."

"I know," Leah said, and inside, she felt braced for the challenge.

When Jackie's car had disappeared down the street, they returned to the living room, arms comfortably wrapped around each other's waist. Butch scampered in and settled onto her bed with a contented sigh.

Leah squeezed Jackie. "Look at the painting now. If you want me to I'll go and get the others and burn them."

"Don't be silly." Jackie let go of Leah and knelt in front of the canvas. After a minute she stood up again. "It isn't me. I don't look like that."

"You do."

"No — I'm not that — I'm not attractive like that. The paintings at the gallery, they weren't me either."

"That's how I see you." Leah put her arms around Jackie's shoulders.

"Artistic license."

"No." Leah shook Jackie gently. "That's how I see

you. If you don't believe it, then you don't believe I
love you."

Jackie looked up, her eyes shining.

♥ ♥ ♥ ♥ ♥

"Ladies, you've got to be grim. Really grim."

"I can't be grim," Jackie said. "I'm a fully
licensed architect recognized by the State of
California as of today's mail."

Leah squeezed Jackie's shoulder. She whispered,
"What do you think he'd do if I used this pitchfork
on him?"

Jackie snickered.

"Grim, think horrible thoughts, ladies!"

Jackie frowned hard. Leah thought it adorable.

"Hold that!" The photographer excitedly snapped
several shots. "Work with me. Frowning's good. You
just got audited by the IRS. Oh, that's very good.
Okay. Let's do some standard shots in your living
room."

Leah gratefully put the pitchfork aside and helped
Jackie unknot her apron. It had seemed a clever
idea — the photographer's suggestion — to stand in
front of her workshop in the same poses and general
appearance as the dour husband and wife of Grant
Wood's *American Gothic,* but standing stock still
holding a pitchfork with the light in her eyes had
been a trial. The photographer's endless good cheer
was also a trial.

"Come on, cover girl," Jackie said, pulling Leah
after her.

They settled on the couch, with Jackie leaning her head on Leah's shoulder.

"Tip your head back. Now, ladies, get ready to smile."

"Something just occurred to me." Jackie glanced up at Leah then looked back at the camera. "Millions of people are going to see us cuddling in this picture. Do you suppose Sharla's parents will see it? Do you think it will change their mind in the slightest?"

"I want to see big smiles, neon smiles. Ladies? Smile!"

Leah chuckled. "I'm pretty sure they don't subscribe to *Vanity Fair*. And they won't change. But maybe someone else will. I tell myself that every time a critic dwells on my 'lifestyle' more than my art."

"Magic smiles! Give it to me! You can do better than that."

Jackie laughed as though she couldn't help herself. Leah swiftly lowered her head and kissed her, then they both faced the photographer again.

"That's it! You're beautiful!"

LOOKING FOR NAIAD?

Buy our books at
www.naiadpress.com

or call our toll-free number
1-800-533-1973

or by fax (24 hours a day)
1-850-539-9731

UNDER SUSPICION by Claire McNab. 224 pp. 12th Detective
Inspector Carol Ashton mystery.   ISBN 1-56280-261-5 $11.95

UNFORGETTABLE by Karin Kallmaker. 288 pp. Can each
woman win her true love's heart?   ISBN 1-56280-260-7   11.95

MURDER UNDERCOVER by Claire McNab. 192 pp. 1st Denise
Cleever thriller.   ISBN 1-56280-259-3   11.95

EVERYTIME WE SAY GOODBYE by Jaye Maiman. 272 pp.
7th Robin Miller mystery.   ISBN 1-56280-248-8   11.95

SEVENTH HEAVEN by Kate Calloway. 240 pp. 7th Cassidy
James mystery.   ISBN 1-56280-262-3   11.95

STRANGERS IN THE NIGHT by Barbara Johnson. 208 pp. Her
body and soul react to a stranger's touch.   ISBN 1-56280-256-9   11.95

THE VERY THOUGHT OF YOU edited by Barbara Grier and
Christine Cassidy. 288 pp. Erotic love stories by Naiad Press
authors.   ISBN 1-56280-250-X   14.95

TO HAVE AND TO HOLD by PeGGy J. Herring. 192 pp. Their
friendship grows to intense passion . . .   ISBN 1-56280-251-8   11.95

INTIMATE STRANGER by Laura DeHart Young. 192 pp.
Ignoring Tray's myserious past, could Cole be playing with fire?
                                               ISBN 1-56280-249-6   11.95

SHATTERED ILLUSIONS by Kaye Davis. 256 pp. 4th
Maris Middleton mystery.   ISBN 1-56280-252-6   11.95

SET UP by Claire McNab. 224 pp. 11th Detective Inspector Carol
Ashton mystery.   ISBN 1-56280-255-0   11.95

THE DAWNING by Laura Adams. 224 pp. What if you had the
power to change the past?   ISBN 1-56280-246-1   11.95

NEVER ENDING by Marianne K. Martin. 224 pp. Temptation
appears in the form of an old friend and lover. ISBN 1-56280-247-X   11.95

ONE OF OUR OWN by Diane Salvatore. 240 pp. Carly Matson
has a secret. So does Lela Johns.   ISBN 1-56280-243-7   11.95

DOUBLE TAKEOUT by Tracey Richardson. 176 pp. 3rd Stevie
Houston mystery.   ISBN 1-56280-244-5   11.95

CAPTIVE HEART by Frankie J. Jones. 176 pp. Love in the
fast lane or heartside romance?   ISBN 1-56280-258-5   11.95

WICKED GOOD TIME by Diana Tremain Braund. 224 pp. In
charge at work, out of control in her heart.   ISBN 1-56280-241-0   11.95

SNAKE EYES by Pat Welch. 256 pp. 7th Helen Black mystery.
                                             ISBN 1-56280-242-9   11.95

CHANGE OF HEART by Linda Hill. 176 pp. High fashion and
love in a glamorous world.   ISBN 1-56280-238-0   11.95

UNSTRUNG HEART by Robbi Sommers. 176 pp. Putting life
in order again.   ISBN 1-56280-239-9   11.95

BIRDS OF A FEATHER by Jackie Calhoun. 240 pp. Life begins
with love.   ISBN 1-56280-240-2   11.95

THE DRIVE by Trisha Todd. 176 pp. The star of *Claire of the
Moon* tells all!   ISBN 1-56280-237-2   11.95

BOTH SIDES by Saxon Bennett. 240 pp. A community of
women falling in and out of love.   ISBN 1-56280-236-4   11.95

WATERMARK by Karin Kallmaker. 256 pp. One burning
question . . . how to lead her back to love?   ISBN 1-56280-235-6   11.95

THE OTHER WOMAN by Ann O'Leary. 240 pp. Her roguish
way draws women like a magnet.   ISBN 1-56280-234-8   11.95

SILVER THREADS by Lyn Denison.208 pp. Finding her way
back to love . . .   ISBN 1-56280-231-3   11.95

CHIMNEY ROCK BLUES by Janet McClellan. 224 pp. 4th Tru
North mystery.   ISBN 1-56280-233-X   11.95

OMAHA'S BELL by Penny Hayes. 208 pp. Orphaned Keeley
Delaney woos the lovely Prudence Morris.   ISBN 1-56280-232-1   11.95

SIXTH SENSE by Kate Calloway. 224 pp. 6th Cassidy James
mystery.   ISBN 1-56280-228-3   11.95

DAWN OF THE DANCE by Marianne K. Martin. 224 pp. A dance
with an old friend, nothing more . . . yeah!   ISBN 1-56280-229-1   11.95

THOSE WHO WAIT by Peggy J. Herring. 160 pp. Two
sisters . . . in love with the same woman.   ISBN 1-56280-223-2   11.95

WHISPERS IN THE WIND by Frankie J. Jones. 192 pp. "If you
don't want this," she whispered, "all you have to say is 'stop.' "
                                             ISBN 1-56280-226-7   11.95

WHEN SOME BODY DISAPPEARS by Therese Szymanski.
192 pp. 3rd Brett Higgins mystery.   ISBN 1-56280-227-5   11.95

UNTIL THE END by Kaye Davis. 256pp. 3rd Maris Middleton
mystery. ISBN 1-56280-222-4   11.95

FIFTH WHEEL by Kate Calloway. 224 pp. 5th Cassidy James
mystery. ISBN 1-56280-218-6   11.95

JUST YESTERDAY by Linda Hill. 176 pp. Reliving all the
passion of yesterday. ISBN 1-56280-219-4   11.95

THE TOUCH OF YOUR HAND edited by Barbara Grier and
Christine Cassidy. 304 pp. Erotic love stories by Naiad Press
authors. ISBN 1-56280-220-8   14.95

WINDROW GARDEN by Janet McClellan. 192 pp. They discover
a passion they never dreamed possible. ISBN 1-56280-216-X   11.95

PAST DUE by Claire McNab. 224 pp. 10th Carol Ashton
mystery. ISBN 1-56280-217-8   11.95

CHRISTABEL by Laura Adams. 224 pp. Two captive hearts and
the passion that will set them free. ISBN 1-56280-214-3   11.95

PRIVATE PASSIONS by Laura DeHart Young. 192 pp. An
unforgettable new portrait of lesbian love . . . ISBN 1-56280-215-1   11.95

BAD MOON RISING by Barbara Johnson. 208 pp. 2nd Colleen
Fitzgerald mystery. ISBN 1-56280-211-9   11.95

RIVER QUAY by Janet McClellan. 208 pp. 3rd Tru North
mystery. ISBN 1-56280-212-7   11.95

ENDLESS LOVE by Lisa Shapiro. 272 pp. To believe, once
again, that love can be forever. ISBN 1-56280-213-5   11.95

FALLEN FROM GRACE by Pat Welch. 256 pp. 6th Helen Black
mystery. ISBN 1-56280-209-7   11.95

THE NAKED EYE by Catherine Ennis. 208 pp. Her lover in the
camera's eye . . . ISBN 1-56280-210-0   11.95

OVER THE LINE by Tracey Richardson. 176 pp. 2nd Stevie
Houston mystery. ISBN 1-56280-202-X   11.95

JULIA'S SONG by Ann O'Leary. 208 pp. Strangely
disturbing . . . strangely exciting. ISBN 1-56280-197-X   11.95

LOVE IN THE BALANCE by Marianne K. Martin. 256 pp.
Weighing the costs of love . . . ISBN 1-56280-199-6   11.95

PIECE OF MY HEART by Julia Watts. 208 pp. All the
stuff that dreams are made of — ISBN 1-56280-206-2   11.95

These are just a few of the many Naiad Press titles — we are the oldest and
largest lesbian/feminist publishing company in the world. We also offer an
enormous selection of lesbian video products. Please request a complete
catalog. We offer personal service; we encourage and welcome direct mail
orders from individuals who have limited access to bookstores carrying our
publications.